A COUNTERFEIT BRIDE

He was going to kiss her.

Her sister's bridegroom was going to kiss her.

She should have stopped him. But she had to play out this fiction, for her brother's sake.

At least that was what she told herself as he closed the distance.

But it wasn't completely true.

She wanted to see what it felt like to kiss a man. And she wanted to pretend, even if only for a moment, that she was just as worthy and desirable as her sister.

THE HANDFASTING

Cover design by Richard Campbell
Formatting by Author E.M.S.

Glynnis Campbell – Publisher
P.O. Box 341144
Arleta, California 91331
ISBN-10: 1938114256
ISBN-13: 978-1-938114-25-0
Contact: glynnis@glynnis.net

Published in the United States of America.

the
handfasting

The Prequel Novella to The Knights of de Ware

OTHER BOOKS BY GLYNNIS CAMPBELL

THE WARRIOR MAIDS OF RIVENLOCH
The Shipwreck (novella)
Lady Danger
Captive Heart
Knight's Prize

THE KNIGHTS OF DE WARE
The Handfasting (novella)
My Champion
My Warrior
My Hero

MEDIEVAL OUTLAWS
Danger's Kiss
Passion's Exile

THE SCOTTISH LASSES
The Outcast (novella)
MacFarland's Lass
MacAdam's Lass

THE CALIFORNIA LEGENDS
Native Gold
Native Wolf

ACKNOWLEDGMENTS

Heartfelt thanks to:

Suzan Tisdale and Kathryn Le Veque
for nudging me to do a holiday novella

My BFF Lauren Royal
for convincing me to find a way to matchmake
my two legendary families

Birthe Hansen for OT brainstorming

Kit Harington and Emma Watson
for inspiration

For all the people who weren't born perfect

and all those wise enough to

see their value anyway

CHAPTER 1

The Highlands
Yuletide 1199

Ysenda hated Yuletide.

All around her, the clan celebrated with feasting and cheering. Lively merrymaking filled the great hall. Laughter and music echoed from the rafters.

Yet she frowned into her half-drained wooden cup.

Her loathing had nothing to do with the supper. Who could complain about the sumptuous food gracing the table each night of Yule? Tonight there were succulent boar's head, smoked mutton, roast venison, rabbit pottage, cockles, hazelnuts, cheese, and endless cups of winter ale.

She didn't even mind the drunken revelry that inevitably followed. Raucous songs chased away the gloom. Lusty lads grabbed at giggling lasses. The music of pipes, harp, and tambors filled the air. Boisterous dancing encouraged the return of the sun after the solstice.

The boughs of holly decking the hall looked admittedly festive. So did the ivy draping the great hearth. Mistletoe hung in all the doorways for good luck. Luminous tallow candles set about the room made the rough wood beams of the keep look warm and welcoming.

For once, despite being crowded elbow-to-elbow into the keep, no one in the clan was bickering. Everyone was freshly-scrubbed, smiling, and dressed in their best finery.

Even Ysenda had made an effort. She'd bathed in lavender-scented water. She'd washed her long linen leine until it was as white as the snow outside. Atop that, she wore her best gown of soft gray wool. Flowing around her waist and across her breast was an arisaid of pale gray plaid, pinned at the shoulder with a silver brooch. Her normally unruly chestnut hair was harnessed by two narrow braids at the crown, tied at the back with a ribbon, and lightly scented with more lavender.

She felt bonnie...almost as bonnie as her sister.

"Caimbeul!" From across the hall, over the top of his bellowing friends, one of the many piss-drunk ruffians snagged a squirming lass by the arm and called out to Ysenda's older brother. "Caimbeul! Why don't ye come dance with Tilda here?"

2

Ysenda stiffened as Tilda pulled away with a horrified blush. Everyone laughed.

That was why she hated Yuletide.

Beside her, Caimbeul grinned at their jest. But Ysenda knew he was dying inside. He wanted so much to fit in, to be like them.

Most of the time, he could pretend he was. Most of the time, Ysenda forgot he was different. When the two of them were alone, he seemed as well-made and fit as any man.

It was only when they were forced to make a public appearance, like at Yuletide—seated beside their sister and father as if nothing were wrong—that his difference was made painfully clear.

Once the crowd gathered and the ale was flowing, the taunts and the laughter began. And to Ysenda's dishonor, their father, Laird Gille, did nothing to prevent the mockery.

Why would he? The laird had disowned his deformed son at first sight. Indeed, the only reason he'd let the boy live was because Caimbeul had been six months old when the laird came home from his travels to lay eyes upon him. Ysenda's fierce mother, descended from the infamous Warrior Maids of Rivenloch, had threatened the laird's life if he touched one hair on her precious son's head.

Beside her, Caimbeul sighed and lowered his half-eaten oatcake. Ysenda followed his gaze. A group of wee lads played beside the hearth. In imitation of their older brothers, they were making fun of Caimbeul's distinctive hobble.

Her grip tightened on her eating dagger as she muttered, "Those sheep-swivin' brats. What do they think they're doin'?"

He gave her a sad, forgiving chuckle. "They're only bairns, Ysenda. They don't know any better."

"Oh, I'd be glad to teach them," she said between her teeth. "Maybe I'll spit them and roast them slowly o'er the Yuletide fire."

That made him smile. "Ach, ye sound like our ma."

"'Tis disrespectful," she insisted. "Ye're the son o' the laird."

In fact, he was the *only* son of the laird. The firstborn. He should be the heir to the clan. But he might as well be invisible. His presence was expected at holiday feasts when the extended clan filled the hall. He was allowed to sit beside Ysenda when the laird flanked himself with his daughters. But Laird Gille paid him no heed. There might as well have been a mile-high wall between Caimbeul and his father.

Still, it was insensitive of Ysenda to remind him of that. She instantly regretted her words.

To make amends and lighten the mood again, she gave Caimbeul a conspiratorial wink. Then, when their father wasn't looking, she used her dagger to steal a slice of roast boar from the laird's trencher, dropping it onto Caimbeul's.

Caimbeul grinned and dug in.

Ysenda couldn't help but grin back. How anyone could overlook the gentle humor in Caimbeul's soft brown eyes—his kindness, his loyalty, his sweet nature—she didn't know. She supposed most people never saw past his crippled frame.

Calling him Caimbeul, which meant crooked mouth, had been polite. To be honest, it seemed there wasn't a bone in his body that was straight. His back was hunched. His spine was shaped like a slithering snake. His hips were twisted. And one shoulder was higher than the other. With each passing year, his deformity had gotten worse, as if the cruel claws of a dragon slowly closed around him, leaving his body more warped and useless.

Most people assumed his brain was likewise twisted. But Ysenda knew better. He might suffer from neglect. But he was bright, and he possessed a wry wit.

Sadly, their father had deemed it a waste to teach him anything. He said the lad would die young anyway, so an education was pointless.

To make matters worse, when Caimbeul was twelve years of age, their warring mother was killed, mortally wounded by a sword. While she lay dying, she made Ysenda swear to look after her older brother. It was no small task for a wee lass of nine. But Ysenda promised she would.

Once their mother was buried, however, things changed. The laird, ashamed of his son's infirmity, banished the lad from the keep. He was sent to live in a wee thatch-roofed cottage in the farthest corner of the bailey.

Looking back, Ysenda had to admit that had probably been for the best. For when the laird was in his cups and Caimbeul was underfoot, their father tended to use his fists, taking out his frustration and rage on the lad.

At the time, however, Ysenda had felt her brother's exile was unfair. And since she'd made that promise to her mother, she couldn't let him go alone. So, heartbroken at the thought of losing both her mother and the older brother she adored, Ysenda stubbornly packed up her things, left the keep, and moved in with Caimbeul.

Her father scarcely noticed her leaving. His attention was fixed on Cathalin, the one daughter who offered him hope. Cathalin was his middle child, the bonnie one, the one who would marry and inherit the lairdship.

Ysenda had done everything she could for Caimbeul. She'd taught him what she knew of reading, writing, and keeping accounts. She'd challenged him to learn about the running of the household and every man's part in it. She'd bribed visiting scholars to tutor him in history and philosophy.

Caimbeul may not have been blessed with a powerful body. But there was much power in knowledge.

And on those occasions when he needed physical defending, it was Ysenda who came to his rescue. She used the fighting skills her mother had taught her. Many a young lad earned a black eye or a bruised shin from daring to mock Ysenda's beloved brother. A few even learned their lesson at the point of her sword.

Caimbeul nudged her with his bony elbow as she slipped him another slice of stolen meat. "Hey." He nodded toward the door with a broad grin. "I think ye've got an admirer."

Ysenda glanced up. A tall, dark, handsome man was staring at her. He wasn't dressed like a Highlander.

Instead of a leine and brat, he wore a long surcoat of deep blue covered by a brown tabard that was belted at the hips. By his brown hooded cloak, he appeared to have just come in from the cold. Snowflakes dusted his broad shoulders and his hood.

A hint of a smile touched the man's lips, alarming her. But that wasn't what made her most uneasy.

The truth was she'd never seen him before.

Ysenda was certain she knew every lad, lass, and bairn in the clan, as well as most of the neighboring clans. She would have remembered this one's face. He was striking, built like a warrior. His hair was the color of coal. His gaze was intense and steady enough to pierce iron.

What was a stranger doing inside the keep?

He lowered his gaze then, and she scanned the room.

He wasn't alone. Half a dozen unfamiliar men were scattered around the hall.

Who were they? And how the devil had they gotten in?

Sir Noël de Ware loved Yuletide.

It wasn't only because the holiday happened to mark his *own* birth as well as the Christ child's. He loved everything about the season. He loved the crèches in the church and the caroles in the hall. He loved feasting on roast goose and drinking spiced wine. Most of all, he loved snuggling up in the wintry weather with a warm woman by a crackling fire.

Which was why he was unhappy.

Instead of enjoying the holiday season in France, he

was stuck here in the frozen Highlands, tracking down a reluctant bride.

King Philip had promised him a wife—the most beautiful lass in Scotland, if rumor was to be believed. Descended from the magnificent Warrior Maids of Rivenloch, she was the heir to a fine Scots holding.

But she'd been delaying him with letters and excuses for weeks now.

She was ill.

She was visiting kin.

The mountain was impassable.

The river was too high.

She was grieving over a lost kitten.

Meanwhile, he'd been stuck in the Lowlands, awaiting word that he could come for her.

Finally, he'd lost patience. He was weary of waiting for the lass to decide that he merited her company.

Part of the King's reason for awarding him a Highland bride was to assure the continuing alliance between Scotland and France. King Philip had recently made peace with Scotland's enemy, England. This had naturally caused a rumble of discontent among the Scots. The fact that this particular Highland bride was delaying their marriage strained not only Noël's patience. It strained the peace between their countries.

So, as archaic as it seemed, Noël decided he'd have to formally demand his bride.

Of course, he was no fool. The Scots might be allies of the French. But Highlanders were a different breed— wild and unpredictable. He couldn't afford to be caught with his braies down in the frozen north. He'd brought only a handful of men with him. He was ill equipped to wage war.

So he decided to use his brains instead of his brawn.

He chose to come at Yuletide. At Yuletide, the castle gates would be open in welcome. The keep would be teeming with people. Ale would be flowing. Spirits would be high. Nobody would be troubled by a few stray faces among the clan.

Once they were safely inside, Noël would announce to the laird that he hadn't been able to endure one more day without his betrothed. With any luck, the romantic gesture would soften his bride's heart. At the very least, with her entire clan as witness, it would make it difficult for her to refuse him.

So far, things had gone to plan. Even now, he and his men were dispersing peacefully through the crowded hall. They'd left their armor and swords outside the gates. There was no need to appear hostile. Still, as a precaution, they'd kept their daggers close at hand.

He scanned the hall and decided that the lass seated at the laird's right hand must be his betrothed.

She was as lovely as he'd heard. Her skin was fashionably pale. Her cheeks were fashionably rosy. Her russet hair was swept up in an amazing labyrinth that must have taken hours to braid. Her chin had a proud tilt. Her stained lips were set in a knowing half-smile. The sweeping neckline of her gown revealed firm, round breasts. Her eyes smoked with subtle, sly desire as she sipped at her ale. She would definitely turn heads, even in France, which was filled with beauties.

Then Noël's gaze drifted to the lass seated on the laird's *left* side. And his heart tripped.

He must have been mistaken. Granted, the first lass was undeniably pretty. But the lass on the left was a maid to take a man's breath away. The rumors were true. He'd never seen a more beautiful female...anywhere.

Her skin glowed with health. Her long auburn hair, shining in the candlelight, fell in simple, gentle waves over her shoulders. She had large, captivating eyes, a pointed chin, and a sweet mouth. The soft wool of her muted gray gown seemed to swirl around her petite body like Highland mist.

As he observed her, the lass stole a slice of meat from her father's trencher. Then, with a crafty grin, she passed it to the man beside her.

The corner of Noël's lip twitched in amusement. It appeared his bride had a streak of mischief in her. That pleased him.

Indeed, as he watched the wayward lass continuing to steal more food right from under her father's nose, an interesting possibility occurred to him.

Noël had always expected to have a marriage of political convenience. Like all French nobles, he served as a chess piece for King Philip. Alliances were often established through strategic marriages. Love had little to do with it. He was just as likely to be wed to a withered beldame or a mere child as to a lovely maid his own age.

Learning that his bride was renowned for her beauty

had been a welcome surprise. But the idea that he might actually grow to *like* this plucky new wife of his? That was quite intriguing.

He kept gazing at her until he caught her eye.

But instead of returning his friendly smile, her grin faded, and she regarded him with suspicion.

Not wishing to make a bad first impression, he quickly averted his eyes. When he next looked up, she'd left her spot at the table and was making her determined way toward him.

He straightened and tossed back the hood of his cloak, prepared to say whatever it took to ensure that he didn't leave the Highlands without a bride. Nothing could prepare him, however, for her bluntness. Or for her big, luminous, soul-searching gray eyes.

"Who are *ye?*" she muttered under her breath in her Gaelic tongue as the merrymaking continued around them. "And what are ye doin' here?"

Noël was taken aback by her fearless and forthright manner. The lass certainly wasted no words. Nor did she seem to be intimidated by the fact that he towered over her by nearly a foot.

"I asked ye a question," she said impatiently.

He fought back a smile. What a brazen lass she was. Noël knew how to speak her language, of course. But it was important that his wife know how to speak French. For over a hundred years, since the Norman conquest, most of the English and Lowland Scots had spoken French, and he planned to take her home to France. So he replied in his native tongue.

"I've come to speak with your father, my lady."

To his satisfaction, she understood him perfectly. But she still stubbornly answered him in Gaelic. "Have ye? Well, ye didn't answer my first question. Who are ye?"

He smiled. Beautiful, mischievous, *and* clever. He was beginning to like the prospect of being wed to such a spirited lass. Indeed, he was tempted to lean down and steal a kiss from her clever mouth.

But he was no fool. He'd been put off already several times. It would be no easy task to get the lass and her father to agree to the marriage. Noël would have to be careful about how he proceeded. So for now, he would defer to her and speak in Gaelic.

"I'd prefer to answer to the laird."

She raised fine, smug brows. "Indeed? And what makes ye so certain he wishes to speak with ye?"

"By my reckonin', he does not," he admitted.

She frowned up at him. Even that expression looked adorable, like the scowling face of a wee hawk.

He gave her a wink and confided, "But I'm goin' to speak with him anyway." Now that his men were dispersed throughout the crowd, he cleared his throat to address the gathering. "May I have your attention, please?"

The musicians ceased playing, and the hall quieted. All eyes went to him. Laird Gille frowned from his seat, looking very much like the wee hawk, before he slammed his cup on the table and rose to his feet.

"Who are ye, and what is the meanin' o' this?"

Noël eyed his men, whose hands rested upon the hafts

of their sheathed daggers. Then he gave the laird a respectful bow.

"My laird, I apologize for interruptin' your revels," he said. "I am Sir Noël de Ware. I've come to claim the bride I was promised by King William o' Scotland and King Philip o' France." He smiled and set a subtly possessive hand upon the shoulder of the lovely lass beside him. "I couldn't stay away a moment longer. I hoped my arrival would be a welcome Yuletide surprise for Lady Cathalin."

Ysenda stiffened. Cathalin? He thought she was Cathalin? How could anyone have mistaken her for her beautiful sister?

From the great table, Cathalin—the real Cathalin— gasped.

Ysenda had heard gossip about Sir Noël de Ware, her older sister's betrothed, for some time now. He was a noble French warrior. He meant to take her sister to France to live with him at his castle. Upon Laird Gille's death, Cathalin would return to Scotland with Lord de Ware to inhabit the keep and rule the clan.

For weeks, neither her father nor Cathalin had been happy about the arrangement. True, there was an alliance between Scotland and France. But Laird Gille didn't trust Lowlanders, let alone Normans. He wanted a Highlander to inherit his land and title. And so he'd ignored the king's command. He'd plotted to hastily marry Cathalin to a Highland laird before her Norman bridegroom arrived.

But the Highlander hadn't yet come.

And the Norman had.

And now he'd mistaken Ysenda for his bride.

Upon hearing Cathalin's gasp, Sir Noël hastened to reassure her. "There's no cause for alarm, my lady. I will take good care o' your sister, I swear." He glanced down at Ysenda with fondness. "I will honor Lady Cathalin and guard her with my life."

There was an uncertain silence in the hall.

Ysenda pulled away from the knight. This wasn't right. Her sister and her father might not want a wedding between Cathalin and Sir Noël. But it was what two kings had decreed. Ysenda would not be a party to such deception, a deception which amounted to treason.

"I'm afraid ye've made a mistake," she told the Norman. "I'm not—"

"Daughter!" her father called out.

For the first time in his life, Laird Gille had wrapped a companionable arm around Caimbeul's shoulders. Caimbeul had a look of confused hope on his face, as if his father had suddenly realized he had a son whom he loved very much.

Only Ysenda noticed the eating dagger that dangled casually from the laird's fingers, an inch from Caimbeul's throat. And there was no mistaking the threat glittering in her father's eyes.

"Cathalin, darlin'," he said, addressing Ysenda. No one in the hall corrected him. Not even Cathalin herself. She only bit her lip and stared intently into her ale. "'Tis no mistake. 'Tis the king's decree. And how fortunate ye are to have your betrothed arrive at Yuletide. The two o' ye shall have a weddin' feast fit for a king."

Ysenda blinked in disbelief. Did her father really believe he could pass her off as Cathalin? Couldn't the Norman see that her sister was the bonnie one? She waited for someone to speak up, to say it was all a jest.

But no one did. No one wanted to contradict the laird. Caimbeul was aware now that his father held a knife to his throat. They both knew if he uttered a word, the laird wouldn't hesitate to make it his last.

Finally, her sister stood and raised her cup, saying pointedly, "Congratulations, Cathalin, dear sister. No one is more deservin' o' this great honor than ye. And no one could be happier for ye than I am."

Ysenda's eyes flattened. No doubt. Things couldn't have worked out better for her sister. It appeared Cathalin would get the Highlander husband she and their father wanted. And Ysenda would be sacrificed to the Norman.

Worse, nobody in the clan was brave enough to come to her defense. She was being thrown to the wolves. And there was nothing she could do about it.

But what was her father thinking? Sir Noël had obviously agreed to marry Cathalin for the title and land that came with her. What would happen when he discovered he'd inherit neither? And what would happen when the two kings found out their alliance had been sabotaged?

It seemed Laird Gille was courting war.

Here and there, the clan folk began to cheer in

tentative congratulations. The laird nodded to the musicians to resume playing. Everyone returned to eating and dancing and making merry, welcoming the Normans to their revels. And her father beckoned Sir Noël forward with an affable wave of his hand.

The Norman offered Ysenda his arm. She didn't dare refuse him, for fear of endangering Caimbeul. So she rested her forearm lightly atop his.

She tried not to panic. Surely her father wasn't serious. He wouldn't *really* defy the king. Surely he'd marry the real Cathalin to this Norman. His proud boasts of finding her sister a proper Highland laird were only that—boasts.

The laird couldn't hide the truth from Sir Noël forever. He must know that the instant Ysenda knew Caimbeul was safe, she'd confess to the Norman that she was not his true betrothed. After all, it was far better to face her father's anger than to invite the wrath of two kings.

Besides, she reasoned as she stole a sidelong glance at the knight escorting her forward, her sister should be grateful. Lots of political alliances were made with doddering old men. At least Sir Noël was fit and handsome. He had broad shoulders and thick, curling hair. His jaw was strong, and his dark eyes sparkled with life. He even spoke perfect Gaelic.

Laird Gille narrowed his eyes at the Norman. "So ye're the one who's come for my most precious prize."

Sir Noël gazed down at Ysenda. The tender sincerity in his eyes made her heart flutter. "I'm honored to have her entrusted to me."

Laird Gille guffawed at that. "I was referrin' to my castle." He picked up his cup of ale with his free hand, the one that wasn't holding a dagger to Caimbeul's neck. "But aye, I suppose my daughter is a prize worth havin' as well." He took a drink, and a foamy trickle dripped down his beard.

Sir Noël smiled at her. "She's even more beautiful than I imagined."

Ysenda's breath caught. He couldn't be talking about her. Had he even *looked* at his real betrothed? Cathalin was flawless. Next to her perfect rose of a sister, Ysenda looked like a common thistle.

By Cathalin's sour expression, she did not appreciate the slight. That anyone would praise Ysenda's looks while Cathalin was in the room was unthinkable. Ysenda could almost see the steam coming out of her sister's perfect ears.

But to be honest, it was pleasant having an attractive man gazing down at her with such appreciation. No one had ever looked at Ysenda like that before. She'd grown accustomed to hiding in the shadow of her breathtaking sister.

Of course, that bewitched look on the Norman's face would vanish once he learned his bride came with no inheritance. But she wasn't going to give him the bad tidings until Caimbeul was out of her father's clutches.

Meanwhile, her brother scowled in frustration. She could see he wanted to help her. But he didn't dare. One slip of the knife, and he'd be good to no one. Her father had been drinking heavily. He might do something foolish, something rash, something he couldn't undo...

"Why wait?" the laird bellowed. "Let's have the handfastin' now!"

Like that.

CHAPTER 2

Sir Noël couldn't have been more satisfied with the laird's idea. Preparing for an elaborate ceremony weeks in advance seemed like a waste of time to him.

The betrothal had been made. The laird had agreed to the marriage. There was already a sumptuous feast laid out at the table. Why not get the deed done?

Besides, he'd seen enough of his bride to suspect there was a splendid body under all that wool. The sooner the wedding, the sooner the bedding.

Then he glanced down at his bride.

A look of sheer panic filled her silvery eyes.

"So soon?" she squeaked.

He placed his hand atop hers in concern. Obviously, haste did not appeal to her. But why?

Surely, she'd been prepared to be a wife. It should come as no surprise. She'd known about the betrothal for some time.

Did she not find him suitable?

True, he was no golden-haired Adonis. He had a few battle scars. And he'd been told he could sometimes look fierce and menacing.

But he was young and strong, capable of defending a lady's honor. And most women found him attractive enough.

"What's wrong?" he asked her gently.

The laird answered for her. "Ach, she's only an anxious bride. All the more reason to make it quick, aye?"

His bride was growing more agitated. But she couldn't seem to find the words to adequately explain why. "Wait. I'm not... Ye can't... This isn't... Da, please... Don't ye see 'twill only make matters worse if ye—"

"Sir Noël, I should introduce ye to your kin," the laird interrupted. He turned to his second daughter, who sat fidgeting beside him. "This is Cathalin's sister, Ysenda."

"My lady, 'tis an honor." Noël made a slight bow.

The laird swung an arm out toward a red-bearded bear of a man. "That's my sister's son, Cormac." He pointed to a smaller version of Cormac. "And that's Dubne, his brother." He waved a hand toward three curly-headed maids who were whispering together. "And those wee gossips are her daughters—Bethac, Ete, and Gruoch."

"Ladies." Noël inclined his head. "Gentlemen. I'm pleased to make your acquaintance."

He lost track of all the kin. Most of them were short and sturdy. Most of them had reddish-brown hair. And most of them were half-drunk. Finally he turned his attention to the young man around whose neck the laird's arm was locked and waited for an introduction. "And ye?"

"This? This is Caimbeul."

Noël could see there was something amiss with the lad. His body was woefully misshapen. But that wasn't all. Distress furrowed the young man's brows. Maybe it was because the laird was waving his dagger about, dangerously close to the man's throat.

"Caimbeul," Noël repeated.

"Sir," the man tightly replied.

Before the laird could continue, his bride interrupted. "Da, please listen to me." Her words spilled out like the falsely calm surface over a turbulent river. "I think 'twould be best if we delayed at least till the morrow so ye can—"

"Nonsense, daughter," the laird chided. "Can ye not see how eager your bridegroom is to have ye by his side?"

"But—"

"And he's come all the way from France."

"Aye, but—"

"I'll hear no more of it. 'Tis best ye're wed right here and now." Then he turned till he was almost nose-to-nose with Caimbeul. "Wouldn't ye agree?"

Noël's bride lowered her head then. But it wasn't in submission. Her eyes were darting about madly, as if she were trying to come up with a clever ploy.

"My lady?" Noël said softly in French. "Is this not your wish?"

She lifted her eyes. They possessed all the colors of a winter sky, shifting from ominous pewter to stormy gray to serene silver. How pleasing it would be to look into those eyes every day for the rest of his life, watching their changing hues and moods.

Then she looked back at her father, who still had a possessive grip on Caimbeul.

"Da, please. Don't—"

"Ye'll do as I say, lass," the laird scolded. "Ye know your place. We all make sacrifices. Look at poor Ysenda here. Even if the unsightly wench somehow manages to snag a husband..." He paused, his eyes twinkling, and Noël was certain the laird must be jesting. The lass was almost as beautiful as her sister—even when she frowned, as she did now. "'Twill probably be no better than a Highland sheepherder. But ye... Ye'll be the wife of a Norman lord. Ye'll be Lady Cathalin de Ware."

Noël's bride clenched her hand atop his now, digging in to the muscle of his forearm. "But Da, the king will—"

"Hush! I'll hear no more!" her father interrupted as he tightened his grasp on the man, hugging him closer. "Ye should be more like Caimbeul. He knows when to hold his tongue. Don't ye, lad?"

Caimbeul lowered his eyes in anger and shame. The hand atop Noël's arm clenched even tighter.

Noël wasn't sure what was going on. Did Caimbeul object to the marriage? The man had been seated beside his bride. Was it possible he had feelings for her? And did she return those feelings? Perhaps she preferred the sweet-faced Scottish lad, despite his crooked body.

Surprised by the pang of jealousy that shot through him, Noël suddenly longed to whisk his bride away from

22

this place. He didn't like the idea of anyone else desiring his wife.

He didn't like Laird Gille either. Didn't like the fact he seemed to be irresponsibly drunk. Didn't like the way he kept cutting his daughter off. Or how he was manhandling Caimbeul. In fact, until the laird died and surrendered his keep, Noël would just as soon remain as far away from the Highland holding as possible.

But to his own amazement, more than anything, he wanted to please his bride.

He spoke for her ears alone. "My lady, is somethin' amiss? Do ye find marriage to me repulsive? Are ye afraid o' me? I won't beat ye, I promise." Then he thought of something else. "Are ye afraid o' the marriage bed? Is that it?"

He saw that calculation in her eyes again, as if she were winnowing wheat from chaff. She turned to him with new determination.

"Aye," she decided. "That's it. I'm afraid o' the marriage bed." There was an eager light in her eyes now as she clutched his sleeve in both hands. "So if ye vow not to bed me tonight, I'll go through with the handfastin'."

She was up to something. He could see that. He doubted the intrepid lass was afraid of *anything*. But though her notion didn't please him—already his body stirred with desire for her—if it was what she wanted, he supposed he could wait another day.

"As ye wish," he said.

Ysenda sighed in relief. She'd bought herself a day. No handfasting was official until it was consummated. Hopefully, in the morn, when her father was sober, he'd realize what a grave mistake he'd made and correct it. Their sham of a marriage would be nullified, and Cathalin, the *real* Cathalin, would take her place as Noël's bride.

Part of her was not happy about that. Already she could tell that Sir Noël was too good for her sister. Cathalin was selfish and spoiled, accustomed to getting her way. Noël was considerate, noble, and polite. He'd likely try to accommodate her, and she'd end up running him ragged.

Cathalin would never appreciate his gentlemanliness. She was used to forceful Highlanders who took what they wanted. She would probably mistake Noël's kindness for weakness and belittle him at every turn.

It was a pity really. But Ysenda could say nothing about it. She was the youngest daughter, without power and without a voice.

Her father still had a dagger at Caimbeul's throat. He obviously didn't expect Ysenda to go through with the ceremony willingly.

But now that she had the Norman's promise—and she trusted the word of a noble knight—she knew she was safe, at least for tonight. So she'd oblige her father and recite the damned handfasting vows.

The ceremony would be brief, doubtless briefer than the lavish weddings of France. Highlanders had little use for religion and no patience for church approval when it came to unions. Matrimony was achieved simply by mutual consent.

Sir Noël's men made a formidable appearance as they gathered round him. They were large and powerfully built. Their manner was grave and guarded. Ysenda thought they looked ready to unsheathe and do battle if anyone so much as cocked an eye at them.

She wasn't sure why, but that gave her strange comfort.

Sir Noël had brought the marriage agreement with him. One of his men unfurled it across the table between the roast venison and the smoked mutton, along with a quill and ink. Sir Noël penned his mark on the document, as did Laird Gille.

Ysenda swallowed hard. The heavy black scrawls on the parchment made the marriage seem all too real…and permanent.

Before the ink was even dry, Laird Gille stood at the table to preside over the rite, and the hall again hushed.

"Join your right hands," he directed.

Sir Noël faced her and clasped her right hand, which felt dwarfed within his. She could feel the calluses that marked it as the sword hand of a seasoned warrior. His palm was warm and dry. She feared her own was sweaty. Yet there was something reassuring in his grip.

"Here," her sister offered, tugging a long scarlet ribbon out of her hair and passing it forward. "To make it fast."

Her father wrapped the ribbon around their joined hands, binding them loosely together.

Then she lifted her face to look at her bridegroom. She

was startled. In the low light, she'd assumed his shadowed eyes were brown. But standing this close, she could see they were actually blue—a blue as deep as the ocean, as dark as the falling night. For a moment, she only stared at him, lost in the heaven of his gaze.

And then she saw he was waiting uncertainly as the silence dragged on.

"Say your piece, lad," Laird Gille urged.

A tiny furrow formed between Noël's brows. Ysenda realized he didn't know the vows for a handfasting. They probably had no such thing in France. It was up to her then.

Her voice shaking, she began. "I, Lady Ysen—" Heat flooded her cheeks as she recognized her blunder. She coughed to cover the mistake, whispering to Noël, "Forgive me. I'm a wee bit anxious." Then she cleared her throat and began again. "I, Lady Cathalin ingen Gille, Maid o' Rivenloch, take ye, Sir...Noël de Ware...to my wedded husband, till death parts ye and me. And thereto I pledge ye my troth."

She gulped. That hadn't been so difficult. And yet those simple words held such great weight.

His voice sounded much surer than hers. "I, Sir Noël de Ware, take ye, Lady Cathalin ingen Gille, Maid o' Rivenloch, as my bride—"

"To my wedded wife," she corrected in a murmur.

"To my wedded wife...till death...comes..."

She fought back a giggle. "Till death parts ye and me."

"Till death parts ye and me..."

"And thereto I pledge ye my troth," she prompted.

"Aye," he said, finishing with a triumphant smile. "And thereto I pledge ye my troth."

"'Tis done then," her father said in satisfaction, clapping the matter from his hands.

Ysenda hardly heard him. Her attention was riveted on the man before her—the man who had somehow, improbably, just become her husband. A warm twinkle glimmered in his eyes. His smile was captivating. And the thumb he stroked softly over the top of their joined hands sent a curious tingle through her veins.

The laird raised a cup of ale in salute, and the clan followed with cheers.

But Noël wasn't finished. He held his hand out to the man on his left, who placed a gold ring in his palm. Unwinding the handfasting ribbon to free her hand, Noël then gently slipped the ring onto Ysenda's third finger.

She stared down at it. It was heavy, carved with the figure of a wolf's head.

"'Tis the great Wolf o' de Ware," he told her.

She bit her lip, troubled by its scowling face. The ring was loose on her finger. She hoped that it wouldn't slip off, that she wouldn't lose it, for it rightfully belonged to Cathalin.

He bent his head down to murmur, "I vow, my lady, from this time forward, ye shall have the protection o' the Wolf."

For one foolish moment, she wished that could be true. She wouldn't mind having an army of fierce wolfish knights at her beck and call.

She gave him a faltering smile, which he returned with

a wide grin that made her heart skip. But this was Cathalin's husband, not hers. And part of her burned with envy at that truth.

He was still clasping the fingers of her right hand when he lifted his left hand to cup her cheek. He tipped her head up, commanding her gaze. His dark eyes sparked at her like a smoldering coal. She had trouble drawing breath. His thumb brushed at the corner of her mouth, coaxing her lips apart. In a sensual daze, she let her jaw relax as her eyes lowered to his tempting mouth.

He was going to kiss her.

Cathalin's bridegroom was going to kiss her.

She should have stopped him. But she had to play out this fiction, for her brother's sake.

At least that was what she told herself as he closed the distance.

But it wasn't completely true.

She wanted to see what it felt like to kiss a man. And she wanted to pretend, even if only for a moment, that she was just as worthy and desirable as her sister.

When he touched his lips to hers, the cheering clan seemed to fade away. There were only the two of them, connected by their joined hands and their searching mouths. Her eyes fell closed. His light breath upon her cheek sent a current of pleasure rippling through her.

And then he leaned closer, increasing the sweet pressure.

She expected, by his formidable appearance, that his kiss would be rough and aggressive. But the warrior somehow reined in his strength. His lips were soft, tender, and deft. His fingertips gently caressed the sensitive flesh beneath her ear, making her shiver.

As he kissed her, he entwined the fingers of his right hand with hers and drew her closer, until their tangled hands formed a lover's knot between their hearts. Ysenda felt like warm candle wax, melting into him. Her heart beat forcefully against her ribs. A quiet, joyful moan sounded in her throat as he inclined his head to deepen the kiss.

Noël never wanted the kiss to end.

It was mad—the strong, inexplicable attraction he felt to his new bride. His heart was pounding. His mouth was ravenous. He didn't dare ponder what was happening below his belt.

He supposed he should withdraw soon. He wasn't even sure public kissing was proper among the Highlanders. Yet he couldn't pry himself away.

Lady Cathalin was irresistible. Soft and sweet, young and lovely, passionate and willing.

She was the best Yuletide gift he'd ever received.

What he'd done to deserve such a treasure he didn't know.

But she was his now.

And he didn't plan to ever let her go.

CHAPTER 3

I t took the taunts and jostling of his men and the clan to break them apart at last. But when Noël, hot and breathless, peered down at his bride, she appeared as stunned as he felt.

Her cheeks were flushed. Her silvery eyes were glazed with desire. She lifted trembling fingers to her rosy lips. If he hadn't been holding her by the hand, she might have staggered backward in dizzy surprise.

The thought gave him immense pleasure. One corner of his lip curved up as he gazed down at her. He fought the powerful urge to whisk her off her feet, carry her up the stairs, and claim his husbandly rights at once.

But he'd vowed he would not—not tonight. And if there was anything that defined the Knights of de Ware more than their healthy appetites for women, it was their honor.

So he leashed the beast in his braies and stepped back with a respectful nod of his head.

"Eat! Drink!" the laird encouraged. "Ye'll need strength tonight, lad, to wield your braw claymore." He made a nasty gesture that caused a roar of raucous laughter and made his new bride blush.

Noël, with a sudden surge of protectiveness, clenched his jaw. No one—especially not her own father—should speak so crudely in the presence of a lady.

But he didn't wish to upset her more, so he wouldn't challenge the laird for his lack of courtesy. Still, he was inclined to pack up his wife and his men and leave the keep at once.

He settled for guiding her to her place at the table and seating himself between her and her father, where he could shield her from the drunken laird's vulgarity. The last thing a skittish bride needed was more fuel for her fear.

And more delay.

Noël might agree to put off the consummation of his marriage by a day. But more than that was bordering on unreasonable. He wanted to get home. Besides, if his wife *did* harbor feelings for that young man, Caimbeul, it was probably best to make a quick, clean break of it.

Still, he knew he couldn't leave until their wedding was official. And so he intended to employ his considerable powers of seduction to ensure that, come tomorrow night, he'd bed a very willing bride.

Ysenda was still reeling from that earth-shaking kiss when Caimbeul leaned toward her, clearly upset.

"Oh, sister, why?" he whispered in despair. "Why did ye do it? Why did ye agree to marry him?"

She rested a comforting hand on her brother's forearm. "Caimbeul, I couldn't let ye be hurt."

He looked miserable. "I'd rather die than have ye wed to a stranger."

"'Twill be fine. Ye'll see," she promised in a murmur, hoping she was right. "The Norman has vowed not to touch me tonight. The handfastin' won't stand. On the morrow, Da will see the error of his ways. He'll realize he can't defy the king. 'Twill be undone faster than ye can blink."

Caimbeul didn't look convinced, especially when he glanced past her at Sir Noël. But he nodded. "Promise ye won't let him touch ye."

She gave him a scheming grin. "I'll sleep with a dagger in my hand."

But Caimbeul didn't return her smile.

In the next moment, her attention was drawn away by Noël's men. As if by magic, they'd produced a cask of wine. Noël said it was the finest from Bordeaux, which he wished to share with his new clan.

Ysenda was impressed, both by the gesture and by the wine. She'd never had wine before. In the Highlands, they drank cider, ale, and, on special occasions, mead.

Noël filled a cup for the two of them to share. She took a sip of the ruby-colored liquid. It was clear, smooth, and sweet. It was also quite strong.

She handed the cup back to Noël. He clasped his hands over hers to drink. His callused palms were warm on her knuckles. She felt that warmth travel along her arms, up her throat, into her face.

Perhaps the wine was stronger than she thought.

He gazed at her as he swallowed. His midnight blue eyes sparkled with delight.

After he lowered the cup, a droplet of red wine lingered on his lips. Ysenda fought a wild urge to steal it with a kiss. Thankfully, he lapped it up before she could do something so reckless.

His hands were still wrapped around hers on the cup. And she was in no hurry to cast them off.

"Do ye like it?" he murmured, lowering his smoky gaze to her lips.

She gulped. "Aye."

His lip quirked up into a wry smile. "Would ye like more?"

Oh, aye, she thought, gazing at his delicious mouth. She'd like much more. More of his smiles... More of his kisses... More...

"Cathalin?" he prompted.

She blinked, then nodded, startled by the strange name and by how quickly astray her thoughts had gone.

But she didn't dare let them wander. This was her sister Cathalin's husband, not hers, no matter what vows they'd exchanged. She'd do well to remember that.

Silently toasting her serious intentions, she downed the second cup all at once.

Noël chuckled in amazement. "Ye *do* like it." Then he curved a brow in warning. "But beware, lass, 'tis a wee bit stronger than what ye're used to."

She licked her lips. It *did* seem as if her skin was growing rather hot.

He refilled her cup a third time, giving her a coy wink that made her heart race.

Her sister was damned lucky. She hoped Cathalin realized how lucky she was.

Ysenda glanced over at her. Somehow, despite the haughty lift of Cathalin's brow and the knowing smirk on her lips, she was still beautiful. Ysenda wondered if she ever looked ugly.

Sighing, she lowered her eyes to her wine. Her father was right about one thing. One of his daughters was probably going to wed a grizzled old sheepherder. And it wouldn't be Cathalin.

"Are ye not pleased, *cherie?*" Noël asked.

Cherie. He'd called her *cherie.* And the concern in his furrowed brows was sincere.

Damn! It wasn't fair that demanding Cathalin was going to win such a prize. Men like him should be loved and adored, not scorned. She felt sorry for the sweet and noble knight.

"I'm fine," she assured him, instinctively touching his chest in pity. When she realized what she'd done, she tried to pull her hand back. But he caught it and clasped it against his chest, over his heart.

"I am yours, *cherie,* heart and soul, from this day forward."

Maybe it was just the wine, but his words made tears gather in her eyes. How she wished that could be true. And how she wished she could hold on to that promise forever.

He gave her hand a gentle squeeze. "I want nothin' more than to keep ye happy."

Her heart melted. Bloody hell. Her sister was going to make mince out of the poor man.

It startled Noël to realize that what he'd said was true. He wanted to please his new wife. He wanted to watch her lovely gray eyes light up with joy and see her pretty pink mouth widen in a smile.

He wasn't the sort of man to believe in love at first glance. But there was something about his bride that bewitched him.

Meanwhile, she was draining her third cup of wine with astonishing haste, like a warrior bracing for battle. He feared the wee lass would drink herself into oblivion if she wasn't careful.

He gently took the empty vessel from her and set it on the table. Maybe a bit of fresh air would clear her head.

"Would ye like to go out?" he whispered.

"Out?"

"Outside."

"'Tis night." Her brow creased. "'Tis wintertime."

"Ye don't strike me as the kind o' lass to be put off by a wee bit o' darkness or snow. And I've got a cloak to keep us warm."

Her eyes sparked as if he'd asked her on a forbidden adventure.

Without waiting for her reply, he took her hand and nodded toward the door. "Let's go."

Most of the clan were too distracted to note their departure. Caimbeul, however, had his scowl fixed on them. Noël gave him a nod that acknowledged the man's disapproval. But that didn't stop him from taking his bride's hand and stealing out the door into the night with her anyway.

The air was crisp and cold. The snow had stopped falling. White drifts draped the ground like a linen sheet. Noël swirled his woolen cloak over his bride's shoulders as they stepped into the courtyard.

She hesitated, glancing down at her feet. He realized she was wearing soft slippers meant only for the great hall.

Without hesitation, he swept her off her feet and into his arms. She gasped, clinging to him as if she feared he'd drop her. But she was no heavier a burden than his chain mail. He sauntered easily across the courtyard, past the outbuildings nestled against the bailey wall. His boots squeaked in the newly fallen snow.

"I suppose 'tis hard to think o' leavin' the place o' your birth," he said. "But I think ye'll grow to like France. And we can return here now and then if it pleases ye."

"That's very kind."

He smiled. "So tell me, what should I know about this land we're to inherit?"

Noël knew the Highlanders followed curious customs. One was that the oldest daughter could inherit the land and become laird in her own right. His brothers had shuddered at the notion. They'd warned him that ere long, his wife would be wearing trews and he'd be forced to don a kilt.

But the idea didn't trouble him. He'd always admired capable women. In fact, he was looking forward to sharing the responsibilities of the holding, particularly since he knew so little about clan life.

"The land?" She wrinkled her brow in thought. "Well...centuries ago, 'twas settled by Vikings."

"Vikings? Invaders?"

"Nae. They were peaceful enough. They came mostly to build homes. Indeed, many o' my ancestors came from Viking stock."

"I see."

"There's little left o' their settlement now, just a few stones here and there."

"What about the land? Does it provide well for ye?"

"Aye. There are fish in the loch and game in the forest—enough to keep the clan fed all winter. We keep sheep, cattle, and chickens. And we sow oats and barley. When summer comes, there are wild berries everywhere." She thawed just a little when she mentioned summer, relaxing against him.

"I'd like to see it in summer."

"'Tis a bonnie time. The braes are cloaked in green grass and wildflowers." Then a crease touched her brow. "Though they're also full o' ankle-bitin' midges."

He chuckled. "What's your favorite place?"

"My favorite?" She mused for a moment. "The Viking well, I suppose."

"The well?"

"'Tis an old stone ruin. But some say 'tis enchanted."

Noël felt enchanted himself. His bride fit into his arms

as if she were made just for him. Her voice was soft and compelling. Her body felt warm and yielding against his. "Enchanted? And why is that?"

"Accordin' to ancient legend, two lovers hid in the well from those who would prevent their marriage. A storm arose, and the lovers drowned. They were cursed to live apart in the afterlife. But 'tis said that at Yuletide, if two lovers tie together locks o' their hair, weight them, and toss them into the well, the spirits o' the ones who drowned will bless them with magic, bindin' their souls together for eternity."

"Is that so?" Noël didn't believe in magic. Everything he'd won, he'd earned—not by magic, but by the sweat of his brow. Still, he didn't want to dampen her spirits. "And is the legend true?"

She shrugged. "I wouldn't know."

"Maybe we should go and try it."

She stiffened in his arms. "Now?" She cleared her throat. "Nae, 'tis late. And 'tis too far away. There may be wolves about."

Noël knew a feeble excuse when he heard it. He might have fallen in love with his bride in an instant. But that didn't mean she shared his sentiments. He'd just have to be patient and win her affections in time.

"Perhaps on the morrow?" he asked.

"Perhaps."

Ysenda knew she should be cold. The air was frosty. The clouds were thick. There was a dusting of snow on all the tree branches. But she felt pleasantly cozy, tucked into the knight's arms, enveloped in his cloak, snug against his firm chest.

She could feel the flush in her cheeks. Whether it was from the Bordeaux or the fact that a handsome man was carrying her across the courtyard, she wasn't sure.

But when she suddenly succumbed to the irrational desire to steal a kiss, she blamed the wine.

It happened in an instant. In one moment, they were speaking reasonably, discussing the history and resources of the land. In the next, she pulled herself up by the edges of his cloak and pressed her lips to his.

Despite surprising him, he responded with levelheaded calm. Then, as if she'd done nothing untoward, he kissed her back.

After that, Ysenda—knowing full well she had no right to do it, no claim on him whatsoever—took his head between her hands and deepened the kiss.

The liquid warmth of their tangled tongues seemed to melt the icy night. Their fervent breaths mingled, making white mist against the black.

Suddenly, her hands were acting of their own will. Her fingers spanned his wide shoulders. They caressed the cords of his neck. They wove through the thick locks of his hair.

He pulled her closer. The pads of his fingers pressed into her back. His mouth ground against hers, tasting of wine and lust. And she liked the flavor.

"Ah, *mon dieu, cherie,*" he muttered between kisses.

As they continued feasting on each other, he tilted her

body, letting her slip down to stand atop his boots. He took her head tenderly in his hands. He tipped up her chin, brushing his thumbs along the corners of her mouth. Then he drew her lower lip between his own, sucking gently.

Through a haze of desire, she felt his fingers drift down her throat and across her bosom. While he clasped the back of her head in one hand, the other strayed along the neck of her gown. When he delved beneath the linen, she was too delirious with desire to refuse him. And when his hand closed over her bare breast, she sucked in an awe-filled breath at the divine sensation.

She should have pushed him away. She should have clouted him. If she'd been in control of her senses, she would have shoved him into a snow bank to cool his loins.

But she wasn't.

All she could do was float on a heavenly vessel of lust, neither knowing nor caring where she was bound.

"Ah, *mon amour*," he murmured against her mouth. "Let's go inside."

She nodded. Anything that whisked her away from this mad and perilous place would be a wise choice. Once they were inside, surely reason would prevail.

He gave her breast one last fond caress. Then he picked her up and carried her swiftly toward the keep.

Luckily, she could blame her ruddy lips and cheeks on the cold weather, though no one paid the couple much heed as they came in. Everyone was too busy passing around the Bordeaux.

Ysenda's breast still tingled where Noël had touched her. But her gown was safely in place. She'd checked it three times to be sure.

Sir Noël excused himself for a moment to confer with her father. The laird pointed up the stairs toward Cathalin's room, and Noël nodded.

Ysenda swallowed hard. This was not going to be easy.

Her brother glowered at her, as if he could read her mind.

She glowered back.

He shook his head.

She stuck out her tongue.

Unfortunately, Noël turned at that moment and caught her in the childish gesture. She quickly withdrew her tongue, but not before his face split into a grin.

She'd hoped their escape to the bedchamber would go unnoticed. But it was not to be. Four Frenchmen gathered round with great pomp to carry Noël on their shoulders. And before she could protest, two more had hoisted her up. With the clan cheering in noisy celebration, the couple were carried up the stairs and deposited before Cathalin's chamber.

Noël opened the door. Ysenda, unwilling to risk further humiliation, hurried in. She counted herself lucky his men didn't push their way past her to make themselves welcome in the bedchamber. Noël waved goodnight to the celebrants and secured the door.

The room was dim. While she stood beside the door, he hung up his cloak and crossed to the hearth, using the poker on the wall to jab the banked coals to life.

Then he added a few chunks of peat to keep the fire going.

It had been a while since Ysenda had been in this chamber. Living in her cottage, she'd forgotten how luxurious the castle was. The carved wood bed was fitted with a thick pallet of feathers and draped in a deep blue brocade canopy. A heavy chest containing Cathalin's gowns crouched at its foot. A large wooden trestle table stood against one wall. Its top was littered with vials and jars of the oils, powders, and potions Cathalin used to maintain her beauty.

The window was shuttered at the moment. But she knew it afforded a magnificent view of the distant brae and the forest where the old Viking well stood, because once, this chamber had belonged to Ysenda as well.

While she was lost in her thoughts, Noël came up behind her. When his hands settled lightly on her shoulders, she jumped.

He chuckled. "I didn't mean to frighten ye, lass."

"I'm not frightened," she scoffed. It wasn't quite the truth. But showing fear was never wise. At least that was what her warrior mother had taught her.

He slid the edges of his thumbs along the tops of her shoulders. "I'm beginnin' to suspect ye're not frightened of anythin'."

He was wrong about that. At the moment, she was a bit frightened of herself.

"Ye made me a promise," she breathlessly reminded him. "I'm trustin' ye to be a man o' your word."

"I'm a de Ware," he said, as if that should explain everything.

Then he turned her in his arms to face him, holding her in his indigo gaze. "But ye know ye can only bend a man so far. I'm your husband now. On the morrow, I won't take nae for an answer."

She nodded. His demands were perfectly reasonable. But by morn, everything would be sorted out. And tomorrow night, in this very chamber, he would claim his husbandly rights...with her sister.

The idea turned her stomach.

Her eyes lowered to his mouth. She couldn't abide the thought of Cathalin kissing Noël. Her brat of a sister didn't deserve to wrap her arms around his neck, to taste his sweet lips.

While she continued to stare, his mouth curved up in a slow, sly smile. "Go on then."

"What?"

"Kiss me."

"What?"

"I can see ye want to."

Flustered, she gave her head a wee shake.

"Go on," he urged, crossing his arms over his chest. "I won't even kiss ye back."

Kissing him again would be a mistake. She knew that. Yet she lowered her gaze to his mouth, considering the idea.

"Come on, lass. I can't wait forever," he teased.

On the other hand, this might be the last kiss she ever got...at least until she married whatever coarse and smelly sheepherder her father lined up for her.

It was that depressing thought that convinced her to take the chance while she had it.

"I suppose I can give ye one kiss goodnight," she decided.

"O' course."

"But only one."

His eyes twinkled with laughter. "Whate'er ye can spare."

Resting her hands on his crossed forearms, she rose onto her toes. She lifted her chin and closed her eyes. He lowered his head to meet her halfway. When she felt his faint breath upon her face, she moved toward him until their lips touched.

If this was to be her last kiss, she wanted to remember it. So she focused on the supple warmth of his lips and the coarse brush of stubble on his chin. She inhaled his masculine fragrance—all leather and iron and spice. Daring to let her tongue venture out, she savored the tempting taste of his mouth. She sighed against him with bittersweet longing.

And then he began to respond.

His mouth moved over hers, gently at first, and then with more urgency, as if he sought to drink the last bit of her before she was gone.

She too was filled with a strange desperation—a craving for more of him, for all of him. A soft moan of longing built in her throat. Frustration creased her brow.

His arms came unfolded. He pulled her into his embrace.

It was utterly thrilling.

It was also dangerous.

"Ye're...kissin' me...back," she cautioned between kisses.

"Am I?"

"Aye."

"Should I stop?"

She paused. "Nae."

Chapter 4

Scarcely realizing what she did, Ysenda began gliding her hands beneath his surcoat. His collar bone was hard and smooth under her fingers. His pulse beat forcefully at his throat. The muscles of his chest flexed beneath her touch. She slid her palms outward. The garment loosened, slipping from his massive shoulders.

Encouraged by her boldness, he rewarded her in kind. He tugged the neckline of her gown lower and lower until it perched precariously on the tips of her breasts.

When their tongues began to entwine, she lost all hope of propriety and control. An erotic vibration began in her ears, blocking out the voice of reason. She pulled at his clothing, eager for his flesh.

He growled inside her mouth like a hungry, wild beast. And she let him feed upon her. She leaned against him, yearning to be closer. At last he pushed her sleeves down, baring her breasts so he could press his warm skin to hers.

It was heaven—this feeling—and she never wanted it to end. Where their naked flesh made contact, it seemed to melt together. Their tongues mated, creating the most intoxicating ambrosia.

She let her hands roam over him with abandon. They swept across his sleek muscles and delved into his lush hair. She tried to memorize every inch of him with her fingertips.

It wasn't enough. She wanted more.

Breaking away from his mouth, she left a trail of kisses...from the corner of his lip...along his jaw...down the side of his neck where his pulse pounded.

He groaned and then sucked a hard breath between his teeth. He drew her closer, until she could feel the rigid length beneath his tabard.

She should have been appalled. Such a blatant display was improper, crude, disgusting. Yet disgust wasn't at all what she felt as he pressed against her.

Instead, a heady thrill coursed through her, as if the Bordeaux filled her veins, warming her blood and making her drunk.

She'd done that. *She'd* made him harden like that.

But wrapped up in her exhilarating triumph was also her surrender. Her bones were melting. Her heart was softening. Her resolve was weakening.

She didn't mean to retreat toward the bed. Somehow it just happened. Suddenly the back of her knees made contact with the wooden frame.

Noël, in his eagerness, continued to advance, covering her face with kisses, not realizing she had nowhere to go.

They toppled together onto the feather pallet.

In the small sliver of her mind that wasn't drunk on wine and desire, Ysenda knew she should resist him.

But a bigger part of her mind knew there was no hope of return. They'd leaped into the raging sea and were being carried away. And every sense she possessed told her to seize the moment.

So she did.

When he was a lad, one of Noël's brothers had tricked him into sitting astride an unbroken horse. The steed had bolted off across the countryside, taking him on a wild ride. And all he could do was hang on for his life.

Which was how he felt now.

He'd resigned himself to spending a tame and quiet evening with his new bride, convincing her with reasonable examples that he'd make a decent husband.

But when she began kissing him, his good intentions went right out of his head.

It wasn't as if he'd never been kissed. He was a de Ware, for heaven's sake. But he'd never been kissed with such passion, such enthusiasm, such genuine enjoyment.

It was his clumsiness that made them fall onto the bed. And once he was horizontal, it was hard to resist doing what came naturally any time he was horizontal with a woman in a bed.

Still, he tried to resist her.

But when the lovely lass began putting her hands on him—clutching at his tabard, tearing at his surcoat—she was difficult to ignore. When she rained feverish kisses all over his face, he was compelled to answer them. And when she rolled him onto his back, all his self-control vanished.

Afraid of the marriage bed?

Hardly.

His new bride was clearly no trembling novice. He wondered what game she played, trying to make him believe she was.

Perhaps she feared he wouldn't wed her if he found out she wasn't a virgin.

She needn't have worried on that account. Noël had always preferred voracity to virtue.

He chuckled low in his throat as she moved her hungry mouth along his collar bone. Now that he knew the truth, he couldn't help teasing her a bit.

"I thought ye said just one kiss."

"Did I?" she said breathlessly.

He grinned. No longer concerned about keeping a rein on his lust, he tangled his hands in her glorious hair and opened her mouth with his. He let his tongue dance on her lips, then plunge within, relishing her wine-sweet flavor.

It had been months since he'd lain with a lover. Once he'd learned of his betrothal to Cathalin, he'd sworn off coupling with other women.

But he was paying for his abstinence now. He was as hard as stone. Indeed, he felt as if he might explode at any moment.

Which would be a mistake. Nothing would disappoint

a bride more than discovering her new husband spilled his seed quicker than a twelve-year-old lad.

So taking a sobering breath, he rolled her over, sitting back on his knees to straddle her so he could have more control. He slipped his hands beneath the neckline of her gown and slid it down past her shoulders, leaving kisses along the way. Then he pulled her garments lower, to her waist, trapping her arms beside her.

"Ye're so beautiful," he murmured. "They said ye were the bonniest lass in all Scotland. They were right."

She gasped as he slowly ran the pads of his thumbs down her soft breasts until they rested above her taut nipples.

Noël smiled as she arched up to force his touch, brushing the peaks of her breasts against his thumbs. Then he lowered his head to replace his thumb with his tongue, flicking lightly at each nipple before drawing the lovely nubbin into his mouth.

She groaned and clenched her fists.

Desire surged between his legs. But he had to temper his lust, at least until hers matched his.

He glided his hands slowly up her silken legs, raising her skirts. She lifted her head and jerked her arms as if she might try to stop him. But her hands were caught in her sleeves. And judging by the smoldering gray smoke of her gaze, he could see she didn't truly want him to cease.

Sure enough, when his fingers crested the tops of her knees and continued upward, she dropped her head back onto the pallet with a sigh of rapture.

When he reached the crease of her thighs, he pushed back her gathered skirts. There he stole a glimpse of heaven. Dark, curling hair made a small, perfect triangle against her fair skin. His loins ached with longing as he perused her lovely body.

Swallowing back his ravenous desire, he gently urged her legs apart. Slipping his fingers into her nest of curls, he opened her as tenderly as a flower.

Ysenda sucked a sharp breath between her teeth. Why was she letting him do this to her? She didn't know. But she couldn't form the words to stop him. Nor did she want to.

She wanted this.

Nae, she didn't want it. She *needed* it.

Yet it wasn't hers to have. He didn't belong to her.

Still, she wanted him so badly.

And when she felt his mouth upon her...down there...all rational thought abandoned her. Stricken by erotic lightning, she could form no words. His lips caressed her with delicious intimacy, flooding her with heat. His tongue bathed her with care, making her gasp in blissful wonder.

She squeezed her eyes closed, too ashamed of her own pleasure and weakness to face him. But her shame came with a curious joy. A powerful force began to build within her. Her veins filled with brilliant fire. Her blood surged with glorious energy. Her flesh warmed and swelled and longed.

Just when she thought she would burst with craving, the world seemed to stop for a timeless instant. Then, with a silent scream, she lost control.

She was rocked by waves of ecstasy as the most divine sensation encompassed her. It seemed she sailed along on a deep ocean of pleasure.

But it lasted for only a moment.

And then he plunged into her.

She cried out, feeling the sudden searing heat of his trespass like a knife.

Noël bit out a curse and froze. What the devil?

He'd been so sure his new bride was not a virgin.

Ah, god, he'd made a terrible mistake. An unforgivable one.

"Oh *non, non*," he lamented. "I'm so sorry, *cherie*."

Her knuckles were white. Her eyes were tightly shut. And her lips were compressed into a tense line.

He ached with remorse. He'd give anything to undo what he'd done.

But he couldn't.

All he could do was to withdraw and leave her alone, as he should have done all along...as he'd promised her he would.

Yet if he withdrew, it would only make things more difficult. The next time, she would be even more reluctant, and with good cause.

That was no way to start a marriage.

Nae, if he wanted to repair the damage he'd done, he

had to help her through the pain and bring her back to pleasure. So he remained within her.

"I'll make it better," he promised, smoothing the hair back from her troubled brow. "I didn't mean to hurt ye, lass. Truly I didn't."

He tugged her sleeves off, freeing her arms. Her hands relaxed. But she still wouldn't look at him. And it broke his heart. He had to fan the flames of her desire quickly before his own subsided.

"Ye aren't afraid, are ye?" he asked. "Because if ye are..."

That got her attention. She opened her eyes and furrowed her brow. "Nae."

She *was* afraid. He could see it in the way she sucked her lower lip under her teeth. But she wasn't going to admit it. And he rather admired her for that.

"I can make the pain go away," he said, "if ye'll allow me."

She looked doubtful. Then she gave him a nod.

Holding himself up on his elbows, he lowered his head to kiss her. But this time, he kissed her softly, tenderly. And when she answered too eagerly, he drew back. It was essential this time that she be completely ready.

It didn't take long. Soon she was reaching for him. She clasped the back of his neck to hold him close. She gasped against his throat and arched up until her bosom grazed his chest.

Then, to his relief, she began grinding her hips slowly against him. He closed his eyes as a ripple of desire coursed through his loins. Even a virgin instinctively knew the dance of love.

The sweet friction was almost too much to bear. He clenched his teeth against his release as she sought her own.

When she finally stiffened, opening her mouth in joyous awe, he groaned her name and drove deep within her. Together, they shuddered out their bliss.

For a weightless moment, Ysenda felt like a hawk, soaring high in the sky. There was no more pain, only freedom. Then she dove through clouds of pure pleasure, plummeting down so swiftly that her wings shivered on the air.

It would have been a moment of perfect bliss...if only he hadn't cried out her sister's name.

The word struck her like a slap in the face, snapping her back to reality.

Bloody hell! What had she done?

Noël, utterly spent, sank down upon her, careful to support his weight on his forearms. He heaved a contented sigh against her neck.

"Ah, lass, I'm so pleased to be your husband."

Ysenda gulped, wrapping her arms around him in an awkward hug.

She didn't know what to say.

She couldn't even pretend this was his fault. She'd encouraged him. She'd been the one who had to have that goodnight kiss. If he hadn't kept his promise, it was only because she'd led him to believe she was no longer holding him to it.

He'd done nothing wrong. He'd only made love to the woman he thought was his wife.

But Ysenda had committed a sin. She'd knowingly and intentionally consummated a counterfeit marriage.

"Are ye all right, *cherie*?" he murmured, lifting his head to look at her.

Nae, she was not all right. She'd behaved like a wanton. And she'd stolen her sister's bridegroom.

But she didn't dare confess to him. So she gave him a bleak smile and nodded.

He eased away to lie beside her, still holding her close.

"The next time," he promised, "'twill be better."

The next time? There could be no next time.

She bit her lip. She supposed she was ruined now. But she wouldn't make Noël pay the price for that. On the morrow, when her father came to his senses and handed over Noël's *real* bride, Ysenda would do the right thing, the merciful thing. She'd deny she'd ever bedded him.

The handfasting would be broken. Noël and Cathalin would be free to wed. He'd whisk his new wife away to his castle in France. And Ysenda would probably never see him again.

She glanced over at the handsome knight with the dazzling smile and the kind heart. If he hadn't drifted off to sleep, he would have seen the childish tears gathering in her eyes.

It was silly, she knew. But she wanted him for herself. She didn't care that he wasn't a Highlander. She didn't care that he was Cathalin's. She didn't even care that she had nothing to offer him—no castle, no land, no title.

She'd given him her maidenhood already. And if she believed for an instant that he'd take it, she'd offer him her heart as well...for she was sure she'd fallen in love with him.

As mad as it sounded, it was true. Though she'd known him only a few hours, she knew he was everything she'd ever wanted in a husband. He was loyal, brave, sincere, fair. He commanded the respect of men and earned the admiration of women.

But her heart wasn't what Sir Noël had come for. He'd come for a political alliance. Besides, a man like him could have any maiden he chose. Why would he choose Ysenda when he'd been given the most beautiful woman in all of Scotland?

She turned away and sulked herself to sleep.

CHAPTER 5

Ysenda woke before the sun. In her sleep, she'd somehow wrapped her arms and one leg around her bedmate. She paled, realizing she had to untangle herself both from Sir Noël and from the mess her father had created before it was too late. She also had to make sure nothing bad had happened to Caimbeul.

She carefully extricated herself and glanced at the man sleeping beside her. She couldn't resist a fond grin. One side of his face was distorted where it was smashed into the downy mattress. His hair stuck out every which way, like a tree struck by lightning. His mouth hung open, and great snores issued forth. The noble knight didn't look quite so noble now. And yet his unguarded sleep made her adore him all the more.

How pleasant it would be to wake up each day to such an endearing sight…to hear the reassuring sound of his breathing…to peruse the sculpted contours of his…

She almost choked when she beheld the bold

silhouette poking up the linen sheet. How could that be? How could he be aroused when he was fast asleep?

Her cheeks flaming, she crept out of the bed before things could get worse. She cast one last despondent glance at the man she was leaving behind. Then she left the chamber to seek out her brother.

"Where is he?" she demanded. "What have ye done with him?"

The laird grimaced as her sharp words pierced his aching head. "He's fine." He shooed her away and continued to poke among the kitchen stores for something to soothe the pain.

She found the vial of willow bark extract and shoved it into his hand. "Father, listen to me. What happened last night was a mistake. Ye can't go against the king. 'Tis…" She glanced around the cellar, even though it was too small to conceal spies. Then she whispered, "'Tis high treason."

"Ach!" he scoffed. "The king won't come marchin' all the way up here to enforce one wee marriage." But Ysenda detected a hint of uncertainty in his eyes. "Besides," he said, uncorking the vial and sniffing at the contents, "'tis too late now."

"But that's just it. 'Tisn't too late." She licked her lips, hating to lie. "We didn't…that is…there was a weddin'…but there was no beddin'."

He screwed up his face in disbelief. "What?"

"The handfastin' can be broken now. He'll be free to marry Cathalin."

He stared at her as if she were stupid. "He's not marryin' Cathalin."

Ysenda's heart plummeted. "But he has to. The king decreed it. Ye signed the papers yourself."

"I'm not givin' my land to a Norman, no matter what the king decrees."

"But my laird...Da...don't ye see? Ye've been given a second chance."

He narrowed his eyes. "Ye wily wench. Ye refused him on purpose."

"Aye, I did. I did it for the good o' the clan. I could see ye weren't in your right mind last night. And I knew if I didn't—"

The back of his fist cracked suddenly against her cheek, rocking her head and making her stagger sideways. She caught herself on the shelf, knocking over a row of bottles that clattered on the stones.

She blinked in shock and worked her jaw, making sure he hadn't knocked out any teeth. Her instincts told her to repay him with a solid punch of her own. It wouldn't have been the first time she'd given as good as she'd gotten from a man.

But for once she had to resist the urge.

After all, he was the laird.

He was her father.

And he had Caimbeul locked away somewhere.

"How dare ye speak to me like that," he snarled. "I know what's best for the clan. And 'tisn't havin' a laird that's not even Scots."

She ignored her stinging cheek. Somehow she had to

convince him he was making a mistake. "But Da, he must be a decent man. The king himself chose him. He'll be good to Cathalin and provide for the clan as well as—"

"Nae, 'tis settled." He took a tiny sip from the vial, wrinkling his nose. "Cathalin's bridegroom, her *Highland* bridegroom, is due to arrive any day now. I'll simply say we couldn't wait any longer for their Norman knight, that by the time he arrived, her weddin' had already taken place."

"You'd lie to the king?"

"'Tisn't a lie. 'Tis a stretch o' the truth."

"And what will ye tell Sir Noël when this Highlander arrives?"

"He'll be long gone. Your husband seems very keen to get home." He toasted her with the vial, took a generous swig, shuddering at the bitter taste, then stuck the cork back in. "Ye know, ye should count yourself lucky, lass. In France, ye'll be a proper lady."

"But Sir Noël will find out I'm not Cathalin."

"Not unless ye tell him."

Her thoughts raced. "And what if I tell him now?"

"Oh, I don't think ye'll do that."

"And why not?"

"Because I'm holdin' that hunchback pet o' yours, and ye don't want to see anythin' bad happen to him."

Ysenda clenched her hands at her sides. She wanted to think he was bluffing, that he wouldn't do anything to harm his own flesh and blood. But she knew better. The laird had been wanting to get rid of his embarrassing son from the moment he'd first seen him.

Laird Gille chuckled. "Ye know, ye're just like your ma. Strong-willed and weak-hearted. Don't think I don't know about your sneakin' in tutors to teach that halfwit."

"He's not a…" She managed to stop herself, but only because she knew it was hopeless.

"Ye'll do fine in France. And if ye get too headstrong for Sir Noël's taste, he has an army o' braw lads at his command to keep ye in line."

If he was trying to scare her, it wasn't working. She trusted Sir Noël completely. What she couldn't anticipate was his reaction when he discovered he'd been gulled by her father…and by her, for that matter. Would he believe the truth—that she'd been in fear for her brother's life? And if not, what would he do to exact revenge? Would he toss her aside and demand his true bride? Would he make war on the clan and lay siege to the keep?

A voice came from beyond the door. "Good morrow?"

Ysenda sucked in a quick breath. It was Sir Noël.

Her father arched a brow. "Your husband's callin' ye." He smirked. "Probably comin' for somethin' ye forgot to give him last night."

"Cathalin?" Noël called.

Ysenda winced.

Her father snickered.

"In here," she called back, swinging open the door.

Noël was even more magnificent than she remembered. He'd finger-combed his hair. His face was freshly scrubbed. He was dressed again in his dark blue surcoat, which set off his sparkling eyes.

Unfortunately, he looked nothing like a man who'd

been forced to spend his wedding night in unrequited passion. And the memory of what they'd done washed over her like a warm wave, heating her cheeks.

"Ah. Good morn...son," her father said. Somehow he managed to make the word sound like both an insincere welcome and an insult. He'd never called Caimbeul "son." Not once.

"My laird," Noël replied with a nod. Ysenda got the distinct impression Noël didn't care to call Laird Gille "Father" either.

Already there was animosity between them. If Lord Noël found out that the laird had tricked him, it would get ugly. She couldn't afford to let that happen, not before Caimbeul was safe.

"Have ye broken your fast, Sir Noël?" she asked, taking his hand, eager to separate the two men. "Are ye hungry?"

"Aye." Noël was hungry, to be sure. He wanted to feast on his wife's lovely body again.

His wife. He loved the sound of that. And to think he'd been dreading meeting his Highland bride.

When he'd awakened to find her gone, he feared it might have all been a dream. But the rumpled sheets smelled like her—fresh, warm, and womanly—and that scent had stirred him to life.

Now, walking beside his lovely new wife, he had to resist the urge to sweep her up the stairs, toss her onto the bed, and make love to her...all day long.

"There should be bannocks in the bakehouse," she said, ushering him out the door of the great hall.

The courtyard was still covered in white. But the sun had peeped out this morn. Icicles dripped from the thatched roofs of the outbuildings. The snowy expanse twinkled like crystals.

His bride was still in her slippers. So he scooped her up to carry her toward the bakehouse.

She squeaked, startled.

He grinned down at her. Then he noticed something that made his smile vanish. One side of her face was red, as if someone had clouted her.

He stopped walking and tipped up her chin to examine the mark. He clenched his teeth. "Your cheek—did someone strike ye?"

She frowned, tugging her chin away. "Nae," she told him. "I probably just slept on it."

He suspected she wasn't telling him the truth. "Ye know that I'm your protector now." Indeed, he was surprised by just how fiercely protective he felt. "If anyone touches ye, he'll have to answer to me."

Her eyes went all soft and dewy when he said that. But he was serious. Any man who laid a hand on a defenseless woman deserved to be beaten to a bloody pulp.

"'Tis very chivalrous," she said. "But ye know *I* come from a long line o' warrior maids."

"So I've heard."

Still, he had a hard time believing his wee wisp of a wife could fend off a grown man. If someone *had* struck her—and he suspected it might be her father—perhaps it was a good thing he was taking her away from this place.

He carried her to the bakehouse. As she'd promised, there were oat bannocks, fresh out of the pan. They were warm, buttery, and filling. He ate three of them. But he saved his last bite for her. He fed her from his hand, letting his fingertip linger on her lip.

He'd appeased one hunger, but the other still nagged at him. He stared at her beautiful mouth. Then, not caring whether it was proper in Scotland, he pulled her close, lifted her chin, and placed a soft kiss on her lips.

She responded at once, letting her eyes drift closed. Her lips were pliant beneath his as she dissolved against him. He pulled her closer, reveling in her warmth. Her arms traveled up around his neck. And then he felt a strong surge of lust in his braies, one he had trouble concealing.

She gasped lightly, and he knew she felt it as well. Without another word, he finished the kiss, nodded to the baker, picked up his bride, and headed back to the keep.

Thankfully, no one stood in his way—not her unpleasant father, not Noël's knights, not the Caimbeul lad. He climbed the stairs and pushed open the door to her chamber.

Then he stopped. Her sister was there, rummaging through Cathalin's clothes.

"Oh!' she exclaimed in surprise, looking back and forth between the two. "I...I just needed to...borrow a gown...from Cathalin. Is that all right...Cathalin?"

Ysenda had never felt more awkward. There was no question now. They were all conspiring together to fool the Norman knight. When he found out...

She glanced at him and gulped. Considering the breadth of his chest, his powerful muscles, and the formidable men who followed him about...she didn't want to be there when he found out.

But there was nothing she could do about it now. As far as Cathalin, it seemed that as long as her sister was granted access to her extravagant gowns, she wasn't in the least perturbed that Ysenda might be swiving the man who should have been *her* husband.

"Cathalin?" her sister prompted again.

"O' course," Ysenda said. "Help yourself."

She gave them a knowing smirk. "I can come back later if—"

"Nae," she said. "We're only—"

"Aye," Noël said simultaneously. "Come back later."

Cathalin left with a wink, coyly waving the stockings she'd picked out.

This was a disaster. Ysenda had still hoped she could persuade her sister, if not her father, to see reason. Surely Cathalin wouldn't wish to be the target of two kings' wrath. But now it would be impossible to convince her sister that she'd never consummated the handfasting.

Noël didn't seem to note her distress. He had only one thing on his mind. And the longer Ysenda gazed into his smoldering azure eyes, the more she had to agree that nothing else seemed important.

What started as feathery, inviting kisses grew urgent and demanding. Against her better judgment, she began caressing his flesh and then grasping at his clothes. By the time they tumbled headlong onto the bed, they were already half undressed.

She told herself it didn't matter if they made love again. After all, they'd consummated the handfasting. What difference did it make whether they coupled once, twice, or a dozen times? A lie was still a lie.

But the truth was she was too overwhelmed by desire to think straight. She wanted him. She wanted this. And when Noël peeled off his surcoat and tossed it aside, the sight of him left her breathless.

There was no time for the play in which they'd indulged last night. They both knew what they needed. There was no reason to delay.

He pushed up her skirts and smoothly sheathed himself inside her. She welcomed him with shivering desire.

This time it felt like they were running together up the slope of a great brae. They panted with exertion as they neared the top. When they reached the peak, they paused to admire the beautiful glen below. Then they tumbled down the other side as fast as a waterfall, rushing over the rocks and diving into a deep, refreshing pool.

Afterward, as they caught their breath, Ysenda thought she'd never felt as contented as she did, lying in Noël's arms. A brilliant glow seemed to surround them, protecting them from regret and guilt and sorrow. She closed her eyes and enjoyed the peace of utter satisfaction.

But all too soon, it faded away. Then she was left with remorse and worry.

What would he think when he found out she was a pretender? Would he think she was no better than a wanton harlot who had used him for her own gratification? Or just a heartless betrayer?

She bit her lip as an even worse thought occurred to her.

What if he'd gotten her with child?

He leaned on one elbow, gazing down at her with adoration and gratitude, two things she knew she didn't deserve. But she forced a smile to her lips.

"Let's get out o' here," he said with a lopsided grin.

"Now?" For an awful instant, she thought he meant to leave immediately for France.

"Aye." He brushed her hair back from her brow. "Why don't we pack a wee feast, and ye can show me this wishin' well o' yours?"

She let out the breath she'd been holding. Brilliant idea. She needed to get away from the temptation of the bedchamber. There was still a chance that Cathalin would decide to do the right thing and agree to wed her intended husband. Ysenda didn't want to jeopardize that possibility any more than she already had.

Still, it was with great regret that she donned her sister's warmest clothing and boots. She bid a silent farewell to the downy bed and to the ecstasy she would never have again...yet never forget.

Noël knew his men were restless, eager to be home. And now that the handfasting had been sealed, there was no reason to remain in Scotland. If they left on the morrow, there might even be some of the holiday left to enjoy.

He smiled at the thought of sharing his new bride with his family. He couldn't wait to show Cathalin the beautiful Christmas crèches. He wanted her to see the jongleurs performing caroles in the hall. And on his birthday, he wanted to drink warm mulled wine with her beside the fire.

Still, he didn't wish to appear rude to her clan. One day, all of this would be his, and he hadn't even given it a decent inspection. So as much as he'd prefer to lie in bed with his delectable wife all day, he decided he should do the proper thing and make a tour of the land.

Now, as they slogged through the snowy field toward the forest, Noël had to admit he was surprised by just how extensive the holding was. It appeared the king had been quite generous. They'd been hiking for some time.

"How much farther is it?" he asked.

"Not far. Just through those trees, in the clearin'."

Her cheeks were rosy with the cold. Her breath made fog on the air. And her gray eyes shone with excitement. It almost seemed a pity to tear her away from the land she loved so much.

"There," she breathed when they finally reached a small clearing in the wood where stray beams of sunlight seemed to cast glittering gems in the snow.

The well wasn't much of a well anymore. It was a ruin. A winding stream ran into what was left of the stone walls and trickled down the other side. Ferns grew up around the moss-covered rock. Snow-laden pines crowded near, their tops bent inward as if to shield the well from intruders. If Noël didn't know better, he'd say it *was* a magical place.

As they drew near, he saw a curious stone disk sitting askew atop the well. It looked like a dislodged lid.

"There's an inscription on top," she told him. "See the Viking runes?"

"What does it say?"

"'Tis a blessin'. For a quiet journey, joyful days, and strong deeds for Odin."

"Odin?"

"The Viking god." She ran her fingers across the carved runes. "And here it says, 'May your love stay true to your noble heart'."

He nodded. "That sounds like a good blessin'." He drew his dagger. "Do ye think we should try it? Shall we cut locks of our hair and—"

"Oh, nae!" she blurted out. "I don't think so."

Her response set him on his heels. Yesterday he expected her to have some qualms about staying true to a man she'd never met. But they were properly married now.

And they'd made love.

Twice.

"Nae?"

"'Tis just...I guess..." she said, stumbling over the words, "I guess I don't much...believe in wishes."

"Hmm." She wasn't being completely forthcoming with him. But he supposed it didn't matter. Wish or no wish, he intended to stay true to his noble heart. And he intended to keep his new bride so satisfied that she wouldn't even *think* of straying.

He sheathed his dagger, and then peered over the stone lid and into the abyss of the well. It seemed like a perilous thing to leave open. A small child could fall in and drown. *Their* small child.

"'Tis deep," he said with a frown. "If I were laird now, I'd seal it up."

"Oh, ye mustn't do that."

"And why not?"

"Because the spirits will be trapped inside. Besides, at this time o' year, all the lasses toss their wishes in it."

"I thought ye didn't believe in wishes."

"Well, *I* don't, nae," she said, coloring a little. "But the others..."

"I see," he said with a grin. He crossed his arms over his chest. "Ye know, ye're quite bonnie when ye blush like that."

She gave him a teasing push. "I'm not blushin'. 'Tis only the cold."

"Well, I'll have to warm ye then, won't I?" He didn't wait for an answer. He opened his cloak and swept it around her, enfolding them both. "Better?"

Ysenda nodded. She had to admit it *was* better. But not because she was cold. She had the thick blood of a

Highlander, after all. And her sister's fur-lined wool cloak and sturdy leather boots were good protection against the snowdrifts.

It was better because she felt...protected...in Noël's arms.

She could protect herself, of course. Her mother had passed on enough of her fighting skills to ensure that her daughter wouldn't be left vulnerable.

But there had never been anyone to champion Ysenda. She'd fought against the prejudice of her father. She'd battled the arrogance of her sister. She'd defended her brother when he was too weak to defend himself. But she'd always fought alone. No one had ever stepped in and taken her side.

Now, for the first time, snuggled in the arms of this Norman warrior, she felt absolutely safe.

"How long have ye been a knight?" she asked.

"I'm a de Ware. I was *born* with a sword in my hand."

She chuckled and gave him a poke in the ribs. "That must have been painful for your mother."

"Oh, aye, the poor woman had eight of us wee knights."

"Eight? 'Tisn't a family. 'Tis an army."

"France's best," he said proudly. He wrapped his arms tighter around her. "I can't wait to show ye off to my brothers."

He began to rattle off their names, too many to remember, giving a humorous description of each. And with each name, Ysenda grew more and more despondent. They sounded so wonderful. But she was never going to meet them. And she had to face that fact.

Indeed, the reason she wouldn't wish at the Viking well was that she didn't want to indulge in the false hope that she could somehow keep him for herself.

As she watched the stream in silence, her eyes mirrored the well, filling with water. A secret tear trickled down her cheek as she longed with all her heart for that which she couldn't have. Then, ashamed of her selfishness, she quickly wiped it away.

His voice was full of affection as he continued speaking about his family. Meanwhile, the water gurgled over the rocks. The ice at the edges of the rill made soft cracks as it yielded to the sun. Snowmelt dripped from the trees.

Ysenda closed her eyes, wishing she could stay here forever, enfolded in his arms.

She wished a lot of things.

But what she'd said was true. She didn't believe in wishes.

CHAPTER 6

Noël spent most of the morn with his new bride, hiking across braes and moors, through the pine forest and past a great loch. They stopped along the way to share the small feast of oatcakes and soft cheese they'd packed, washing it down with cider.

Afterward, she pointed out the best fishing place and the spot where the lasses liked to bathe in summer. She showed him the rotting remnants of a Viking longhouse where she used to play and the holly grove where her mother had once frightened away two wolves. He saw how much she loved the land. It made him love it as well.

But there was also a touch of sorrow in her gray eyes. He wondered... Was it the idea of leaving her home that saddened her? Or something more?

He thought again about the young man who'd sat next to her at the table. They'd seemed very close. Did her heart belong to him? Jealousy pricked at Noël again.

He supposed it didn't matter. They'd journey to

France in a day or two, leaving everyone she knew far behind.

Still, that didn't change the way she *felt.* And Noël wanted his bride to be in love with *him.*

The idea was laughable. He'd come to Scotland for one purpose—to make a political alliance. Falling in love had never been part of his plans.

But that didn't change the fact that he wanted to win her heart now. He wanted to make her smile. He wanted to bring the joy back into her eyes.

"So, lassie, when was the last time ye made a snowwoman?" he asked.

She quirked her brow at him. "I've made a snow*man.*"

"Oh, aye, everyone's made a snowman. But have ye made a snow*woman?*"

She gave him a skeptical grin. "I don't see how there could be much difference."

"What? O' course there's a difference. Come on, I'll show ye."

Together they piled and packed the snow until they had a vertical mound that was about her size. He rounded the top into a ball for a head. She formed two stubs to serve as chubby arms. Then she sought out two small pine cones to make eyes. He made a small snowy nose, and he stuck a curved twig under it, turning it into a frown.

"Why is she so unhappy?" she asked.

"Because she looks like a snow*man.*"

"I told ye there was no difference."

He scowled and stroked his chin, studying the

sculpture. "Perhaps if ye found some beautiful flowin' hair for her."

She perused the glen and found golden drifts of fallen pine needles near the trunks of the trees. While she was busy gathering them, he set to work. He patted together two small globes of snow and plucked a holly berry to perch in the middle of each one. These he affixed strategically to the front of the body. Then he waited for her return.

First she gasped. Then she giggled. It was a delightful sound.

"Shame on ye, Sir Noël," she scolded, unable to keep the laughter from her voice.

"Shame?" he asked, all innocence. "Why?"

Her silvery eyes danced as she came up beside him. "Ye aren't goin' to leave her like that."

"Like what?"

She gave him a chiding elbow. "Undressed."

"She'll be fine," he assured her. "She won't get cold. She's a snowwoman."

"'Tisn't the cold I'm talkin' about, and ye know it."

He reached out and turned the frowning twig into a smile. "But look how happy she is now."

She shook her head. "Ye're a naughty lad."

He winked at her. "Ah. Wait till ye see my snow*man.*"

For a moment, she only stared at him. Finally her eyes went wide, and her mouth formed a shocked "O." She started pelting him with the pine needles.

He laughed and shook off the deluge. Then he caught her about the waist and hauled her to him.

Kissing her felt as natural and instinctive as breathing. Her lips opened to his as readily as a lock to a key. Her laughter spilled into his mouth, and he lapped up her joy. Their tongues touched, and the current bolted through him, making him instantly hard and eager.

If it were summer, he would have spread his tabard on the soft grass and made sweet love to her, right there and then.

But the world was wet and frozen.

So, between kisses, he gasped out, "Let's go back...to the keep...before I turn *ye*...into a snowwoman."

Shaking off his lust, he took her hand and began the short hike home, happy he'd made her smile. But by the time they emerged from the wood, in view of the keep, he was already thinking about her warm bedchamber.

"I'll race ye," he said.

"What?" She giggled.

"Come on. Whoever is first to the gate gets to undress the last."

She was still puzzling out whether it would be better to win or lose when he bolted off across the snow.

"Wait!" she cried. "Ye cheated!"

"Hurry up!"

"But ye never said go!"

"Go!" he yelled.

He gained several good yards. But then he made the mistake of turning around to gloat. While he was running backward, his heel caught on a tree root, and he fell smack on his arse.

She burst into laughter, charging past him as he scrambled to get up.

"Come back here, wife!" he bellowed after her.

"I don't think so!" she crowed.

"But a wife's supposed to obey her husband!"

She only laughed.

Chuckling, he dusted the snow off of his surcoat and let her get a short distance ahead. He was enjoying the view, after all, watching her bustling backside and catching a glimpse of her lovely calves as she picked up her skirts to scurry through the snow.

He couldn't get over the fact that she was his. That breathtaking, vibrant, fresh-faced Highland lass belonged to him. How he'd gotten so lucky, he didn't know. But he didn't intend to let her get away from him. Now or ever.

In the end, he let her win, but only by an instant. He nipped at her heels the whole way, making her squeal in panic one moment and giggle at his antics the next. By the time they collapsed against the gate, they were breathless from running and giddy with laughter.

He grinned into her shining gray eyes and bent to give her a bold kiss, deciding he didn't care whether it was proper or not. What should it matter if a few curious clansmen saw how much he loved his bride?

Her lips were cool. Her tongue was warm. Her breath mingled with his as they kissed, then caught their breath, then kissed again.

"You win," he whispered, cradling her face with his palm. Then he stepped back with his arms outstretched. "Go ahead. Undress me."

She gasped in delighted shock, shoving at his chest. "Ye're a wicked, wicked man."

She'd add a few more "wickeds" if she could read the lusty thoughts coursing through his head right now. Of course, he wasn't about to act on any of them. By now there were several sets of eyes on them.

Instead, he escorted her politely through the gate, walking hand-in-hand with her.

The courtyard was bristling with Yuletide preparations. Cooks roasted haunches of mutton on a great spit. Maidservants tied together clumps of evergreen with red ribbon. Kitchen lads carted baskets of bread into the keep. And in one corner of the yard where the snow had been shoveled away, his men were sparring, providing lively entertainment for the laird and for the wee lads gathered round.

When Noël lifted his gaze, he saw someone else was watching. At the highest window of the tower, intently studying the knights, was Caimbeul.

"They're very good," his bride exclaimed as she saw his men crossing blades.

He smiled. "Aye." The Knights of de Ware were the best swordsmen in France.

He peered up again at the window. Caimbeul had spotted him. The young man was staring back at him with a venomous glare.

Noël frowned. Was that jealousy? He had to find out. He might not be able to mend the lad's broken heart. But he could at least try to make peace with him and make the truth—that Cathalin was his wife now—easier to bear.

"Would ye like to watch them for a bit?" he asked her.

"Aye, if ye don't mind."

"Not at all." Kissing her knuckles and releasing her hand, he glanced up again at the scowling Caimbeul. "I'll be back. I've somethin' to attend to."

Ysenda admired good swordsmen. It was a trait she'd doubtless inherited from her mother. And the Knights of de Ware were far superior to any fighters she'd seen in Scotland.

But that wasn't the real reason she wanted to watch them.

She mostly wanted to avoid going to Cathalin's bedchamber.

Ysenda's will was weaker than ever now. Not only did she desire this Norman knight with the handsome face, unruly black hair, and dazzling blue eyes. But now she also adored him.

He made her laugh. He made her feel beautiful. He made her feel loved.

She glanced down at the Wolf of de Ware ring on her finger. Giving him up was going to be painful. And the more intimate they became, the harder it would be.

Cathalin was watching the knights battle as well. Maybe if Ysenda could get her sister alone, talk to her, she could make her see reason.

After Noël left, she approached.

"Cathalin," she whispered, tugging on her sleeve.

Cathalin whipped her head around. "Don't call me that," she hissed. "They might hear ye."

"We need to talk."

"There's nothin' to talk about."

"'Twill take but a moment. We likely won't see each other again for years. Can we not at least say farewell?"

Cathalin rolled her eyes. "Ach, very well. I've grown weary o' watchin' these French bairns playin' with their wee blades anyway."

Wee blades? Their broadswords might not be as big as a Scots claymore, but Ysenda was sure an agile Norman with a light blade had a definite advantage over a Highlander with a heavy sword.

They retreated to a spot along the back wall of the keep.

Cathalin crossed her arms over her bosom. "What did ye wish to say?"

"I need ye to think about what ye're doin'."

"I know exactly what I'm doin'. I'm marryin' a Highlander. And he and I will inherit the castle and rule the clan when Da is gone."

"But don't ye see? The kings won't allow it. They've betrothed ye to a Norman because they want a Norman to hold the land."

"It doesn't matter if they'll allow it. 'Twill be done. I'll be wed ere they can have their say." She smirked. "Besides, ye've already made good on the handfastin'."

"We can say I haven't," Ysenda said, clutching her sister's sleeve in desperation. "We can say 'twas never consummated. Then ye'll be free to..." She almost choked on the words. "To wed Sir Noël."

82

"I don't *want* to wed Sir Noël."

"Ye must. 'Tis the will o' the king."

"I don't care," Cathalin said with a pretty pout. "Besides, Da said the royals wouldn't dare come to the Highlands to—"

Ysenda grabbed her sister by the shoulders. "They *will* come. They'll send men like those," she said, pointing toward the Knights of de Ware. "And they'll kill everyone in the clan if ye don't do as the king wills."

Cathalin pried Ysenda's hand from her shoulder. "Then ye're goin' to have to keep pretendin' *ye're* Cathalin. 'Tis the only way to keep the peace."

Ysenda sighed in exasperation. "He'll find out. Even if I say nothin', it won't be a secret for long. As soon as Da dies, the secret will be out."

Cathalin straightened with pride. "By then my Highland husband will have raised an army to defend the keep." She scoffed. "His men will slaughter every last one o' these wee bairns with their wee blades."

Ysenda could only stare at her sister, mortified. How could Cathalin be so delusional, so reckless? She would bring destruction down upon their clan. And for what? So she could wed the man of her choice? A man she'd never even met?

She wanted to wring her sister's perfect neck.

But maybe she could try a different approach. Ysenda had no intention of going to France in Cathalin's stead, leaving Caimbeul and their clan behind to be killed by the king's army.

"Ye know, Sir Noël would be a very good match for

ye." The words were hard to push past her throat. "He comes from a wealthy family. Ye'd live in a beautiful castle. Ye'd have everythin' ye desire. Servants at your beck and call. All the new gowns ye want. Jewels, furs, falcons. Sir Noël would grant your every wish, I know. And your bairns... They'd be the most beautiful children in all o' France."

"That may be." Cathalin sniffed. "But I refuse to marry such a blind and stupid man."

She blinked. "What do ye mean?"

Cathalin lifted her haughty chin. "How could the fool have thought *ye* were the most beautiful lass in all o' Scotland?"

While Ysenda stood with her mouth agape, Cathalin picked up her skirts and stalked off in a vexed huff.

Ysenda could only stare off after Cathalin. She couldn't argue with her. That *was* what Sir Noël had thought. And once Cathalin's pride was insulted, there was no way to assuage her feelings.

Hell. Now she didn't know what to do.

Noël rapped lightly on the door. "Caimbeul?"

There was no answer. But he heard a startled scrape on the other side.

He slowly opened the door, preparing to defend himself if necessary.

Caimbeul was sitting on the floor below the window, scowling up at him.

"I need to speak with ye," Noël said.

Caimbeul's frown turned mistrustful.

Noël closed the door behind him. Caimbeul made no move to rise, but perhaps the young man's twisted frame made it difficult for him to stand. He obliged the lad by hunkering down before him.

"I think 'tis best we speak plainly," he told him, "so I'd like the truth from ye. Do ye have…feelin's for my bride?"

Caimbeul's face twisted. "Feelin's? What do ye mean?"

"Romantic feelin's."

Caimbeul's eyes narrowed with rage. Before Noël could dodge aside, the young man shot out a furious fist. Fortunately, it missed Noël's nose, but only because a heavy iron chain around his wrist brought it up short. Still, Noël instinctively recoiled, falling backward onto his hindquarters.

"How dare ye!" Caimbeul yelled. "She's my sister, ye horse's arse!"

Noël didn't know what shocked him more—the fact that Caimbeul packed an impressive punch for a crippled man, that he was chained like an animal, or that he was his bride's brother. He held up a hand in peace.

"Wait. Ye're her brother? The laird's son?"

"Aye," he ground out.

Noël sat forward, resting his forearms on his knees. He remembered the laird's attitude toward Caimbeul at the table. He'd never introduced him as his son. And he'd treated him with a distinct lack of respect.

"Is your father the one who put ye in chains?"

Caimbeul didn't answer. His frown of shame was answer enough.

Why would the laird do such a thing? Was he afraid his son would interfere with the wedding? Maybe Caimbeul thought he was protecting his sister.

"Tell me, man to man," Noël said. "Do ye disapprove o' me? Do ye think I'm not good enough for your sister?"

Caimbeul's eyes burned with silent anger. "Which sister?"

It was a strange question. "The one I'm married to, o' course."

Caimbeul stared at him in silence for a long while, as if deciding whether to say anything further. Finally he did. "Ye're not married to the right one."

"What do ye mean?"

Instead of answering, Caimbeul focused on the ground and said tightly, "Ye've slept with her, haven't ye?"

Noël let the lad's words sink in. What did he mean, "the right one"? Was it possible he'd married the wrong sister?

"She's Cathalin. Aye?" he asked, fearful of the answer.

"She's not."

Noël felt the breath freeze in his chest. How could that be? How could he have wed—and coupled with—the wrong sister?

Then he glanced again at the young man. Perhaps Caimbeul was mad. Perhaps he was confused. Perhaps that was why his father had chained him up.

"Are ye certain?" he asked.

"O' course I'm certain. I know my own sisters. Ye've wed...and bedded," he added with a sneer, "Ysenda, not Cathalin."

Noël couldn't comprehend it all. He rose slowly to his feet. "But why would…"

"My father wanted a Highlander, not a Norman, to inherit his land."

"But 'tisn't up to your father. Two kings have decreed this marriage."

"Aye, and ye've seen it through. As far as ye know, ye're wedded to Cathalin."

"But that's ridiculous. If she's not the real Cathalin, then when the laird dies—"

"Ye'll inherit nothin'. The land will go to the *real* Cathalin and her Highlander husband."

Noël was astounded. "That can't be true. Every member o' the clan would have to be privy to the deception in order for—"

"No one said a word when you mistook Ysenda for Cathalin. They were too afraid to gainsay the laird. My father was overjoyed. Ye played perfectly into his hands."

All the air went out of Noël's lungs. How could this have happened? Had his honest mistake become an act of rebellion? He shook his head, which was spinning as he recalled the events of the past day.

"Your father was afraid ye'd speak out," he realized. "That's why he had a knife at your throat."

Caimbeul nodded.

"And why he's put ye in chains now."

"Aye."

"Then he mustn't know I came to speak with ye." Noël straightened and placed a hand of reassurance on

Caimbeul's forearm. "I don't know how, but I promise ye...brother...I'll make everythin' right."

With that, he left the chamber. But his mind was far from settled. And as he descended the stairs, he began thinking—not like a suitor, but like a warrior.

By offering him the wrong bride, Laird Gille had intentionally broken an oath to two kings. By rights, Noël should drag him before the royal court.

But the clan would turn on him if he made a prisoner of their laird. That was the last thing he wanted to do, considering that some day these people would be his responsibility. He'd always ruled his knights, not by force, but by earning their respect. And that was how he wished to rule the clan.

Besides, he'd only brought a small contingent of his men. True, they were Knights of de Ware. But they were no match for a hundred angry clansmen.

There had to be another way. And he was determined to find it.

Still, that wasn't the most troubling aspect of the deception for Noël. The worst part was knowing his bride had lied to him. She'd held his hand, kissed him, spoken the handfasting vows.

His brow creased as he remembered she'd asked him not to consummate the marriage. Perhaps she'd had one moment of regret then.

But they *had* consummated the marriage. She'd let him... Nae, he corrected, he'd imposed himself upon her. It had been an accident, but it *had* been his fault. Maybe she hadn't wanted for it to happen.

Still, she'd never told him the truth—that she was not his real betrothed—even though there had been ample opportunity for her confession.

She'd laughed with him.

She'd slept with him.

She'd made him fall in love with her.

Was it all a lie? Did she have no feelings for him?

He frowned, swallowing down the lump lodged in his throat.

It didn't matter, he told himself. They were not intended to be husband and wife anyway. He would find some way to annul the marriage. No one had seen them in the bedchamber. He could claim he'd never consummated the handfasting. That way she could continue her life, unburdened by their sin.

But his heart felt like it was breaking in two. He couldn't get her laughing gray eyes out of his mind. Nor could he think about the other sister, the one he was supposed to marry, without a shudder of distaste.

He would do his duty, for king and country, no matter how painful it was. But he would never be happy about it.

CHAPTER 7

Ysenda watched with the rest of the clan as the Yuletide bonfire was lit in the courtyard. Sir Noël stood beside her. The flames illuminated his face. But his expression was still inscrutable, as it had been since he'd returned from the keep. She didn't know what was wrong. Somehow he seemed...distant.

It was probably just as well. After failing to convince Cathalin to do the right thing and marry Noël, Ysenda figured her only hope was to make Noël fall in love with Cathalin. Once he saw her sister in her best light, surely he couldn't help but be charmed by her. All men loved Cathalin. And of course, Cathalin would fall madly in love with him, for what woman would not? Maybe then Ysenda could repair the damage that had been done.

Of course, the whole idea made her sick at heart. She couldn't bear the thought of losing Noël, especially to her spoiled sister. But for the sake of her brother, whom she'd vowed to protect, and for her clan, to whom she owed allegiance, she'd make the sacrifice.

"Ysenda!" she called softly to her sister, nudging her when she didn't respond to the unfamiliar name.

Cathalin scowled.

Undaunted, Ysenda touched Noël's forearm and smiled back at her sister. "I was goin' to tell Sir Noël about the time we tried to save the pups in the pond."

Cathalin stared silently back. Finally she shrugged and said, "Go on then."

Ysenda gave her sister a pointed look. "But ye tell it so much better."

Cathalin sighed. "What's to tell? We saw the pups in the pond, and we jumped in to pull them out."

Ysenda's face fell. "Aye." She turned to Noël to explain. "But 'twas silly, because the mother hound was only tryin' to teach them to swim." She grinned. "We didn't know they could swim, so we dove in to save them. And when Ca-, my sister found out, she was furious, because she got her new gown soakin' wet."

Cathalin managed a small smile then. "After 'twas ruined, I gave *ye* that gown."

"So ye did," Ysenda said with a chuckle.

She glanced at Noël. His expression was one of polite interest, no more.

Ysenda tried again. "Your hair looks lovely tonight, dear sister."

That worked. Cathalin touched her locks. "Do ye like it? It took Tilda half the morn to braid."

"'Tis beautiful. Don't ye agree, Sir Noël?"

He nodded.

Cathalin, clearly annoyed by his lack of praise, pursed her lips.

Ysenda wrung her hands. What more could she do? What would impress Noël?

"Ye know, Sir Noël, my sister is quite skilled with a needle."

Noël lifted a brow. "Sewin' cloth or jabbin' people?"

With a huff of irritation, Cathalin picked up her skirts and whirled away to stand beside someone else.

Ysenda turned to Noël in accusation. "Why did ye do that?"

"She's like a spoiled hound. Someone needs to bring her to heel."

Ysenda thought about his words as the flames flickered high into the night sky.

"Someone like ye," she decided. "Someone who could take her in hand, teach her patiently, bring out the best in her." She gulped. "Do ye think ye could be happy with...someone like my sister?"

His mouth tightened as he stared into the fire. "Not nearly as happy as I am with ye."

Ysenda's eyes filled. She tried to blame the smoke. But her heart was breaking.

"I... I've grown tired. I'm goin' to go up to bed."

She didn't wait for his reply. She needed to get away before she burst into tears. Maybe Noël would speak again with Cathalin. Maybe not. But she would at least give them the opportunity.

After she left, Noël tried valiantly to fall in love with Cathalin. He stared at her from afar in the bonfire's glow, admiring her perfect profile, her creamy skin, her pouting lips. He watched her laugh when someone whispered in her ear. He saw her toss pine cones onto the fire with delicate grace.

But she wasn't her sister. She didn't have Ysenda's honest face, her sweetness, her endearing awkwardness and innocent charm. Cathalin was haughty, coddled, and hopelessly vain. Life with her would be unpleasant.

Noël watched his chance at happiness float away, like one of the bright sparks from the bonfire, rising and becoming swallowed by the black sky. All he could think about was the irresistible lass who waited in her bedchamber even now, less than a hundred steps away.

She'd pledged him her troth. She'd spoken the words to bind them as man and wife. At least, that was what she wanted the world to believe. And if she wished to keep up that appearance, why should he deny it?

If tonight was to be their last night together...if tomorrow he would confront the laird and demand his true bride...then perhaps he should seize what joy he could before he resigned himself to a lifetime of misery.

He gave the woman he was supposed to wed one last glance. She was beautiful. There was no doubt. But she was no match for the lass he'd married.

Against his better judgment, he took those hundred steps to the bedchamber.

When he softly entered the room, his wife was

crouched by the fire, stirring the coals. She shot to her feet in surprise. The flames crackled to life behind her, illuminating the sheer linen of her leine, leaving nothing to his imagination.

"I thought ye were stayin' below a while." Her voice was cautious.

His eyes never left her as he closed the door behind him. "And I thought ye were goin' to bed."

"I was. I am."

This woman had lied to him. She'd deceived him, earning his trust now so she could exploit it later. Worst of all, she'd made him fall in love with her. By all rights, he should feel hurt and betrayed.

But seeing her in the hearth's soft glow—her face alit, her eyes shining, her lips so tempting—made him feel only longing.

Had her affection for him been a ruse? Did she feel nothing for him?

He had to find out.

"Then let's go to bed *together*," he said.

She gulped. "Don't ye want to watch the Yule fire?"

"Nae. I've seen enough." He took a step toward her.

She fidgeted with her gown. "They make a circle round the outside..."

He took another step.

She licked her lips. "And they walk..."

He took a third step.

"In the direction o' the sun, so..."

His fourth step brought him close enough to detect the smoky desire in her eyes. And when he lowered his gaze, he could see the sweet curve between her breasts where the linen gapped away.

"Tell me somethin'," he whispered, almost afraid of the answer.

"Aye?" Her voice cracked.

"Do ye love me at all?"

As she stared up at him, her eyes filled with tears, and her chin began to tremble.

He felt his heart crack. She might not want to say the words. But the answer was there in her silence.

He clenched his jaw against bitter disappointment.

But just as he would have turned and left her alone— perhaps to drown his sorrows in a barrel of Bordeaux— she collided against his chest with a great sob.

"Oh, aye, god help me, but I do, Noël. I love ye so much."

She rained kisses and tears on him in equal measure. The warmth of her admission was a soothing balm to his heart. He held her close, too lost in relief and joy to think beyond the moment.

Their kissing quickly fanned the flames of love from affection to desire, then from desire to desperation. Noël didn't want to think about tomorrow. Or his king. Or his *real* bride. All he wanted was one beautiful night with this irresistible woman who, aye, loved him.

Ysenda knew she was playing a perilous game. Yet she brazenly continued, like the lads who leaped through the Yule bonfire. She couldn't stop herself.

The situation was impossible. She hadn't been able to make Cathalin fall in love with Noël, any more than she could make *herself* fall *out* of love with him.

And now that she'd admitted she cared for him, she couldn't confess that she'd deceived him. It would break his heart.

Yet even as the deadly knot of lies and deception wrapped around her, all she could think about was making love to him. She didn't want to think about her sister. Or Noël's return to France. Or what would become of Caimbeul. All she wanted was to live for this moment.

Somehow their clothes fell away. Somehow they wound up on the bed. In a delicious tangle of limbs, they let the rest of the world disappear.

His lips kissed away her guilt. His fingers caressed away her cares. And with his bare flesh pressed to hers, there was no room for remorse.

She floated in heavenly oblivion. For now, all that mattered were the two of them and their compelling quest for pleasure.

This time, it was more than mere coupling. She wanted to show him how much she cared for him. She wanted him to feel her love in the deepest recesses of his soul. And she wanted to feel cherished in return.

When he pressed gently into her, she sighed in relief. Looking up at him with a languid gaze, she saw the same sweet satisfaction in his midnight eyes.

When he began to move within her, she met him, thrust for thrust. Just as they had hiked hand-in-hand across the snowy fields, they traversed the landscape of desire together.

His gaze burned into hers. His breath sent shivers along her skin. His tongue bathed her with intoxicating nectar. His fingertips teased and coaxed her to greater heights.

Wanting to keep him with her forever, she wrapped her legs around him. She dug her heels into his buttocks, making him groan with bliss.

He laced his fingers through hers, anchoring her to the mattress. She caught her breath as her lust sharpened to a fine point. Then it exploded into a hundred beautiful fragments. She arched up and clenched her fists in his.

He answered her, surging into her with a ragged cry of release.

Then she stiffened.

He'd called her by name.

Her *real* name.

She sucked in a panicked breath, but he wouldn't release her. His fingers were still entwined with hers. And when he slowly opened his lust-glazed eyes, she saw the truth.

He knew who she was.

He knew everything.

For a long moment, they only stared at each other.

"How did ye find out?" she whispered.

He didn't answer her. Instead, his gaze hardened. "How could ye lie to me?"

"I had to," she confessed. "I had no choice."

He was still holding her down. She wasn't afraid of

him, not really. He was a man of honor, a knight who'd never harm a lady. But she could see by the glower in his brow and the strength in his arms that he could be a fearsome foe.

"When did ye plan to tell me?" he demanded.

"I've wanted to tell ye all along. I tried to stop the handfastin'. I never meant to consummate it. I hoped to convince my sister to wed ye." She added quietly, "I still do."

"Why didn't ye just tell me that first night?"

She swallowed hard, lowering her eyes. The truth was humiliating. But she owed it to him. "The laird said if I told ye, he'd hurt Caimbeul. He's been wantin' to kill my brother ever since he was born. He can't abide havin' a son who's…who isn't perfect. When my mother died, she made me vow to look after Caimbeul. I've always taken care o' him."

His fingers loosened around hers. The grim line of his mouth relaxed. "Ye could have told me. Your father wouldn't have known."

She gave him a rueful smile. "And what would ye have done then? Insisted on marryin' my sister? And when my father refused, would ye have taken on the whole clan with your six knights?"

He compressed his lips.

"I never wanted to deceive ye," she told him. "'Tis pure madness to go against the king. I've tried to tell my father so. But he won't listen. He wants a Highlander to hold his lands."

"When the kings find out—"

"They'll send an army to quell the clan. I know. My father refuses to believe that. And my sister thinks her Highland husband will bring men to defend the keep."

"So he'd rather start a war than see a Norman inherit his lands."

She nodded.

He unlaced his fingers and rolled off of her then, lying on his back to stare at the ceiling. She pulled the linen sheet up over her breasts.

It pained her to say the words, but she did. "I wish my sister loved ye."

He didn't hesitate. "I could never love her. Not the way I love ye."

Her heart flipped over. And then it sank. "What are we to do?"

"*Mon dieu,* I don't know."

A good night's sleep solved nothing.

Noël wished he'd never learned the truth. He could have lived happily in France with his counterfeit bride for years before her father died. By then, it would be too late to undo what had been done. Not that he even wanted to. He'd begun to dream less about inheriting the Highlander's land and more about stealing off with the man's daughter.

But, short of kidnapping her, he still didn't know how to solve the problem of his marriage.

One problem he *did* know how to solve. A young lass like Ysenda shouldn't be burdened with watching over her brother for the rest of his life. This morn, Noël intended to prove to her that Caimbeul was not some helpless creature who needed to be hand-fed and fussed over. If Noël could do nothing else, he could at least give Ysenda the gift of freedom.

He crept out of the bedchamber without waking her. Most of the clan were in the great hall, breaking their fast with buttered oatcakes. He approached Laird Gille.

"My laird, I haven't seen your man, Caimbeul, about lately."

The laird grunted. "Why should ye be interested in him?"

Noël shrugged. "I was wonderin' if ye think he'd be up for a wee bit o' sport this morn."

The laird's eyes lit up. "Sport?"

"Aye. My men have issued me a challenge. They say I can't make a fighter out of a cripple. I say I can."

"Indeed?" The laird stroked his beard in speculation. "And have ye put coin on it?"

He waved away the idea. "Nae, 'tis only a matter o' pride."

The laird's eyes were glittering now. "Pride? Ach! There's coin to be made on a wager like that."

"Perhaps."

Laird Gille chortled. "Not to mention it could be an amusin' sight—Caimbeul with a sword."

Noël bit back his distaste. "So do ye think he'll agree?"

"Oh, aye, I can get him to agree."

"After breakfast then? In the courtyard?"

"Aye." The laird gleefully rubbed his hands together and left to fetch Caimbeul.

Noël didn't tell Ysenda what he was up to. She'd only try to interfere, to protect her brother. She'd find out soon enough anyway.

The knights were exercising in the courtyard, and the sun was dancing along the tops of the distant pines when Caimbeul, no longer in chains, came limping and lurching briskly across the yard, leaning on a gnarled staff.

Noël studied him. But instead of noting the flaws in his gait, he looked for the man's strengths.

Of course, Noël's men hadn't really issued that challenge. They knew Noël well enough to realize he could turn any man into a fighter. Instead, they welcomed Caimbeul onto the field with open arms and ready blades.

Laird Gille had servants bring him a chair so he could sit on the sidelines. He probably imagined he was about to see a horrific and entertaining spectacle. A small crowd of men gathered around. Noël could see them exchanging coins, betting on the outcome.

By the time Caimbeul reached Noël, his face was an angry shade of red, and his eyes were full of rage.

"Is this how ye repay me for tellin' the truth?" he bit out. "By makin' sport o' me?"

"Not at all, brother," Noël said in quiet reassurance. "I'm goin' to teach ye to fight properly...so ye won't have to be afraid o' your father anymore."

Caimbeul blinked in surprise. For an instant, hope flared in his eyes. Then they darkened with cynicism. "I'm a cripple. I can't fight."

"Ye threw a fair clout at me last night. If it hadn't been for the shackle, ye would have flattened me."

Caimbeul almost looked pleased at that.

"Come on," Noël urged, clapping him carefully on the shoulder. "Let's show your father what ye've got."

The lad fell a few times. His father laughed. But each time, Noël and his knights bolstered the young man's courage and heart, assuring him he was making good progress.

And he was. He might not have the stature to wield a broadsword with great precision, power, or speed. But he had surprise on his side.

Anyone looking at Caimbeul would imagine he couldn't defend himself. But even with his twisted frame, he could thrust forward with a dagger, cuff a man squarely on the nose, and kick an attacker's legs out from under him.

Indeed, Laird Gille started to frown as Caimbeul managed to not only stay on his feet, but to knock a few of the knights off theirs.

It was then that Ysenda arrived.

But to Noël's chagrin, the wide grin of triumphant pride and cheery salutation he gave her was withered by her scowl of pure fury.

CHAPTER 8

Ysenda's heart had fluttered in panic when she'd awakened to find Noël gone. Had he decided it was too painful to say goodbye? Had he simply left without a word?

Even though that would probably be best—even better if he'd absconded with Cathalin—she hoped with all her heart he had not.

She scrambled to the window and peered out through the shutters. Noël's men were still here, sparring in the courtyard below.

With a sigh of relief, she turned back toward the bed. Her gaze caught on the foolish prize she'd collected last night while Noël lay sleeping—the black curl she'd snipped from his head and tied into the red handfasting ribbon.

She tucked her lip under her teeth. She'd forgotten about that. It had been a childish gesture. But she'd wanted a memento of him.

Someone scratched at the door. With a little gasp, Ysenda snatched up the incriminating lock and stuffed it down the bodice of her leine. She opened the door to Cathalin and her maid, come to choose Cathalin's attire for the day.

After they'd gone, Ysenda threw on her own gown and went downstairs. She meant to make one more attempt to convince her father to make things right. She grabbed a buttered oatcake in the great hall, and made her way outside to speak to the laird, who was watching the Norman knights practice.

Now she'd reached the edge of the field where her father was seated. She halted in her tracks.

What she saw made her jaw drop. She let the oatcake fall to the ground.

In the midst of the fighting stood Caimbeul. He was dragging a sword behind him as he hobbled toward two of Noël's men.

He suddenly swung the weapon around. The first knight dodged it. The second shoved Caimbeul aside with his shield, pushing him off balance.

Caimbeul tumbled backward onto his arse. Beside her, her father snorted in laughter.

Her blood boiled.

Clenching her jaw, she strode forward. She shoved her clansmen out of her way, stealing a sword from one of them before he even realized it, and kept charging.

Caimbeul had recovered now and was back on his feet, hacking away at his attackers. But it would only be a matter of time before he fell again.

She elbowed aside one of Noël's knights. He instinctively drew his blade. Then, seeing she was a woman, he sheathed the sword and backed away with his palms raised.

"To me!" she yelled at the knights attacking her brother.

Like most strangers to the Highlands, the French knights were unaccustomed to facing a woman with a weapon. Startled, they turned to her. One of them lowered his shield. The other was forced to raise his when she came at him with a blow forceful enough to lop off his head—had it landed.

Jarred by the impact of his shield on her steel, Ysenda staggered back a step. But she recovered quickly enough to intervene between the knight and her brother and took another swing.

From across the field, she heard Sir Noël shout, "Nae!"

Too late. She gave his man a punishing clip on the shoulder. He stumbled backward, clutching his bruised arm, while his companion quickly retrieved his shield.

But then she was caught around the waist from behind. Before she could squirm away, her sword was wrenched from her grip. An instant later, her captor swept her off her feet with a swift kick to the back of her heels. Instead of letting her fall, he caught her on his arm and lowered her with exaggerated care onto the wet grass.

She immediately rose on her elbows, scowling up in sputtering rage. But her anger vanished when she saw who had disarmed her.

"Caimbeul?" She blinked in astonishment.

He grinned down at her. "Good morn, sister."

"What did you…? How did you…?"

It seemed impossible.

He gave her a wink. "'Twould appear ye're not the only one whose veins run with the blood o' warriors."

She was still speechless with wonder when Noël hunkered down beside her. His brow was heavy.

"*Mon ange,* are ye hurt?"

She glanced back and forth between the two men. Noël's eyes were filled with concern, Caimbeul's with gleeful pride. "What the devil is goin' on?" she snapped.

"She's fine," Caimbeul assured Noël.

Noël looked doubtful. "'Twas quite a spill she took."

Caimbeul shrugged. "I've seen her take worse."

Noël shook his head. "How can ye bear to watch your own sister fight?"

"She's tougher than she looks."

Noël's brows raised. "Is that so?"

"Oh, aye. And 'tisn't the first time she's fallen on her arse."

Ysenda frowned. "That'll be quite enough, ye two. I'm right here, ye know. I can hear ye."

She struggled to her feet, batting away their helpful hands.

Noël murmured, "Are ye sure ye're all right?"

"I'm fine," she bit out, though her pride was bruised. "Now one o' ye had better tell me what's goin' on."

"Sir Noël's teachin' me to fight," Caimbeul said.

"Oh, he is, is he?"

Her eyes burned as she turned slowly to face Noël.

Then she seized him by the front of his tabard and dragged him out of Caimbeul's hearing. "Teachin' him to fight?" she hissed. "Against battle-tested knights? A...a cripple?" She hated to use that word, but there was no other term for it. "Why? Did ye think 'twould be entertainin' for my father?"

Noël's eyes grew dark. He lowered his cool gaze to rest on her fists, still clenched in his tabard. His unspoken message was clear. He wouldn't allow her to belittle him in front of his men and her clan. And he wasn't going to reply until she unhanded him.

So she did.

But she still needed an answer.

"How could ye be so cruel?" she whispered. "Can ye not see how the laird mocks him?"

"He's not mockin' him now."

She glanced at her father. Noël was right. The laird wasn't gloating. He was glowering.

"Your brother is more capable than ye think. He's more capable than even he believes."

"Ye don't understand. He's...he's crippled."

"He's a wee bit twisted up," Noël admitted. "But he can still fight. He knocked *ye* on your arse." One side of his mouth lifted in a smile.

"Maybe he can trip up his sister. But he can't fight against seasoned warriors." A wave of dread washed over her as she considered the consequences. "If ye make him believe he can, ye'll get him killed."

"And if *ye* make him believe he cannot, ye'll keep him weak."

Her shoulders drooped. "I can't let harm come to him. I made a vow."

His eyes softened. "Ye were children when ye made that vow. He's a grown man now. He can take care o' himself."

Ysenda bit her lip. Part of her wanted to believe that. But Noël didn't know Caimbeul like she did. He didn't see how Caimbeul had been mocked and belittled all his life, how he longed to be normal. He couldn't understand her brother's pain.

"Watch him for a wee bit," Noël suggested. "And if ye don't agree that he can fend for himself, ye can go back to wipin' his arse."

She gave him a shove for that remark, but it only made him grin. Then she peered past his shoulder at Caimbeul, who was already back to sparring with one of Noël's knights. She couldn't remember a time when her brother had looked so bright-eyed, eager, and alive.

It was a difficult decision. But she finally nodded her assent. Noël returned to the field.

Her knuckles were white as she clenched her fists in her skirts, resisting the urge to rush forward in Caimbeul's defense while he dodged slashes from men with arms as thick as oaks. She gasped several times when a blade narrowly missed his head. And her heart dropped to the pit of her stomach when one of the knights sent him sprawling in the grass.

But then, in the midst of the fighting, Noël called out a few instructions. Caimbeul suddenly executed an unexpected spin to duck backward under one man's sword arm, pushing him forward into the second attacker.

As the two knights fell in a tangle of chain mail, Caimbeul crowed in victory. Noël rushed forward to clap him on the back.

"Well done. Ye see? Your best weapon is the element o' surprise."

Intrigued now, Ysenda watched as Noël continued to train her brother with a unique style and technique. Of course, once Caimbeul began to improve and his antics were no longer amusing, the laird lost interest and retired to the keep. But Ysenda remained to watch in fascination, glimpsing a side of her brother she'd never seen before.

Gradually, over the course of an hour, Noël transformed Caimbeul into an impressive and lethal fighter. Even more significant, the Knights of de Ware became Caimbeul's companions in arms. They challenged him, jested with him, boasted and cursed together. Her brother finally had friends who treated him as an equal.

Yet to what end?

Her heart sank. The knights might be his brothers now. But soon they would desert Caimbeul to return to France. Then he'd be left once again with clansmen who mocked him.

It wasn't fair. It was bad enough that she had to surrender a perfect husband to her selfish sister. It was beyond cruel to make Caimbeul sacrifice his happiness as well.

She had never felt more like fortune's foe.

In the shadows of the armory, Noël unbuckled his sword belt and tossed it aside. He was filled with regret. As if choosing between his duty to his king and the dictates of his heart wasn't difficult enough, now he had to grieve over losing a young brother whom he'd quickly come to admire.

Noël had never had a more enthusiastic and attentive student than Caimbeul. The young man not only learned fast, but he was clever and inventive. If only Noël had more time with him, he was confident he could mold him into a respectable warrior.

Noël slipped his tabard off over his head, then bent forward to shiver off his chain mail, letting it pool on the ground.

Behind him, he heard someone enter the armory. The uneven gait—the stab of a staff and the foot dragging across the floor—was instantly identifiable.

"I came to thank ye, Sir Noël," Caimbeul said quietly, "for givin' me somethin' no man's ever given me before." He stopped in the middle of the chamber. "Hope."

Noël's shoulders lowered. Hope? He feared he may have given Caimbeul only *false* hope. What would become of the lad once the knights left? Would he go back to cowering before his father?

"Ye've made me see that I'm more than just a cripple," he continued. Emotion thickened his voice. "I'll never forget that. And I'll never forget ye."

Noël nodded and turned to Caimbeul. But he couldn't look him in the eyes. "I'll never forget ye either."

However, another pair of eyes floated into his thoughts. Eyes that glowed like soft gray fog. Eyes that shimmered like the sleek silver sea. They were eyes he'd never be able to banish from his mind. With a sigh, he sank down on the wooden bench and hung his head.

Caimbeul limped over and sat beside him.

"Ye love her, don't ye?" he guessed. "Ysenda?"

Too weary to lie, Noël nodded.

"And ye don't want to leave her."

Noël swallowed back despair and answered gruffly. "'Tisn't my choice. I'm honor-bound to do the king's will."

Caimbeul shook his head. "'Tis my own damned fault. If I hadn't told ye ye'd wed the wrong sister..."

Noël smile ruefully. "'Tisn't like sparrin', Caimbeul. Ye can't feint and fool and deceive your way through life."

"Can't ye?" he grumbled.

Noël shook his head.

"But if ye truly love my sister, isn't that all that matters?"

Noël clucked his tongue. "Ye've got skills with a blade now. But ye still have much to learn about duty and honor."

Caimbeul heaved a sigh. Then he drew his dagger and began idly carving the top of his wooden staff.

"Besides," Noël said, "would ye not prefer I take the real Cathalin and leave Ysenda here? I know ye're very close to your sister. And she loves ye very much."

Caimbeul continued carving in silence, but Noël saw his lips compress with an unasked question.

"Ye were hopin' to come with us," Noël guessed, "weren't ye?"

Caimbeul shrugged. "Maybe." He dusted the wood chips from the top of his staff. "I could make myself useful now."

His words broke Noël's heart. There was nothing worse for a man than not feeling useful. He wished he *could* take Caimbeul with him.

But if he did the right thing and married the real Cathalin, he had to leave Caimbeul behind. He couldn't be so heartless as to steal Ysenda's brother from her.

With a growl of frustration, he shot to his feet, raking his hands back through his hair.

The abrupt movement spooked Caimbeul, who lurched from the bench in surprise and almost fell. As he grabbed Noël to regain his balance, his dagger grazed Noël's neck.

"Ach!" Caimbeul cried. "Forgive me. Ye startled me. Are ye all right?"

"Aye," he said, clapping his hand to his bloodied neck to make sure his head was still attached. Then he gave the lad a wink of reassurance. "'Tis only a scratch. But ye'd better put away your weapon before your warrior blood gets the best o' ye."

"Sorry." Caimbeul sheathed his dagger and bent to retrieve his dropped staff. "Are ye sure ye're all right?"

Noël sighed. Nae, he was *not* all right. He was brokenhearted and discouraged. He could see no way out of this predicament. There would be no happy ending...for anyone.

After Caimbeul limped off and Noël was alone again in the armory, his thoughts began to drift.

The Viking well suddenly materialized in his mind. Why, he didn't know. He didn't actually believe in enchantments. Only a fool would imagine an ancient ruin held some magical power.

Yet Ysenda's words haunted him. What had she said? That the well could bless two lovers, binding them together for eternity.

Which was ridiculous. But he supposed every place had its local legends—the Highlands probably more than most. For the superstitious, all it took to keep such a legend alive was enough inexplicable coincidences.

Noël, however, was neither superstitious nor gullible. Shaking his head over his absurd imagination, he left the armory.

As he entered the great hall, he glimpsed Ysenda near the far wall. She looked as beautiful as...as a Viking goddess.

He frowned. A Viking goddess? What had made that pop into his mind? He knew nothing about Viking goddesses.

He straightened and made his way through the crowd toward Ysenda.

Her smile was melancholy. Her eyes looked like heavy clouds about to loose their store of rain as she murmured, "I can't thank ye enough for what ye did for Caimbeul."

"He's a good fighter. If he puts his mind to it, he'll one day be a great Viking warrior."

"A what?"

Noël furrowed his brows. What had made him say that? "Highland, a great Highland warrior."

Ysenda's eyes were moist. He could see his praise of her brother meant a lot to her. But the longer he looked at her, the more miserable he felt. Standing beside her was torture when he knew he couldn't keep her.

He had find an excuse to get away, if only for a moment.

There was a keg of ale at the opposite side of the hall.

"I'm goin' to fetch myself a drink from the well. Would ye like me to get one for ye?"

She gave him a quizzical look. "From the well?"

"What?"

"Ye said ye were fetchin' a drink from the well."

"Nae, I didn't."

"Aye, ye did."

Had he said that? What was wrong with him? "I'm fetchin' a drink from the keg there, on the far...wall. Aye, that's what I said, from the wall."

That wasn't what he'd said, and he knew it. But he couldn't explain why his mind was fixated on that damned Viking well. And he didn't want to try.

Without waiting to see if she wanted a drink, he left to fill two cups.

By the time he brought her ale back, he'd forgotten all about the well. He nodded toward her father. The laird was speaking to three of the de Ware knights and Caimbeul.

"It looks like your father has new respect for his son."

"Aye," she replied, taking a sip, "at least while he's surrounded by your men."

The reminder of Noël's imminent departure brought a scowl to his face.

Just then, Cathalin breezed down the stairs and into the great hall. Not a hair was out of place. Not a wrinkle creased her gown. Even his own men, accustomed to the great beauties of France, turned their heads as she entered the room.

But looking at her only made Noël's heart sink. A weight descended on his shoulders. And he knew he had to do something about it.

"We need to talk," he told Ysenda.

"I know."

"We need to decide what to do. I planned to leave today, and—"

"Today?"

"Waitin' any longer won't make it easier."

"I know."

She was trying to be brave. He could see that. But her eyes were wet. And it was making his throat ache.

A tendril of her hair fell forward against her cheek, and he brushed it back, tucking it behind her ear. But his gaze locked on it in speculation.

A lock of her hair and a lock of his, tied together with a ribbon.

He frowned. He was *not* going to do it. It was a silly ritual. A waste of time.

And yet, he thought as she clamped her jaw to keep her chin from trembling, what harm would it do? He'd tried everything else. Why not try this? As long as no one caught him at the well, no one would be the wiser.

But how would he get a lock of her hair?

"And who will ye be leavin' with?" she choked out. "My sister? Or me?"

She was on the verge of tears. He knew she didn't want to cry in front of her clan. So he took her hand and guided her toward the stairs.

When they reached the shadows of the stairwell, he swept her into his arms. He kissed her deeply, passionately. It was a bittersweet embrace of loss and longing, of fond farewell and ill-fated desire.

It was also an opportunity for Noël to sneak out his dagger and steal a wisp of her hair. Feeling foolish, he nonetheless managed to collect it without her knowledge. He closed it in his palm and then broke off the embrace to hold her at arm's length.

"I need to be alone for a wee bit...to think."

She nodded.

He looked into her eyes again, imparting his love for her with a glance. And then he left.

CHAPTER 9

After he'd gone, Ysenda's eyes filled and spilled over. Sobs lodged in her throat, too painful to swallow away.

She never wept—at least not where anyone could see her. Weeping was a sign of weakness. Or so her mother had always believed. So she sat on the step, indulging her sorrow in secret.

Was there no way to undo what had been done? Was there no choice that would satisfy everyone? Was there nothing she could do to change their destiny?

As she continued sniffling into her hands, she felt an itching between her breasts. With tear-damp fingers, she reached into her bodice.

The lock of his hair. She'd forgotten it was there.

She withdrew it by the red ribbon and stared at it. Suddenly a strange tingling started at the back of her neck. A wee hope blew through her soul like a stray wind.

Locks from each lover's hair, tied together with a ribbon.

Was it possible? Could she call upon the magic of the Viking well?

She didn't even know if she believed in the magic. Some of the clan swore by it. But she didn't put much faith in old legends and ancient enchantments.

On the other hand, something had compelled her to snip the lock of his hair last night. Why else would she have done that? She must have known, deep in her heart of hearts, that she would end up visiting the well.

She ran her thumb over the silky strands of black hair. She was being childish. It was only a Yuletide story, after all. Nobody even knew if the story was true. Going there was probably a reckless waste of time.

Still...what was the harm? She had to try.

Wiping away her tears, she went upstairs and donned her cloak. She didn't want Noël to see her going. He would guess what she was up to. And he would think she was a fool. So she left the keep quietly and took a roundabout path to the well.

Halfway there, she stopped to rest. Drawing her dagger, she cut off a small piece of her own hair and tied it together with his. Her auburn and his black made an interesting contrast. She couldn't help but think about what their children's hair might look like.

She gulped. What if a child was already growing in her belly? The thought was at once thrilling and horrifying.

Closing the precious strands in her hand, she

continued on her journey, hoping no one would catch sight of her.

In fact, she was so busy making sure she wasn't followed that when she arrived, she didn't notice at first that she wasn't the only visitor to the well. A mere ten paces from the stream, she finally saw she wasn't alone.

She gasped in surprise.

Noël glanced up with a frown. "Ysenda?"

"What are *ye* doin' here?"

He hid something behind his back and cleared his throat. "I could ask ye the same thing."

She realized she was holding the bound locks of hair where he could easily see them. But she couldn't exactly tuck them back into her bodice. "I needed...fresh air."

He wasn't fooled for an instant. And his gaze went immediately to what she was holding in her hand. "What have ye got there?"

A dozen lies crossed her mind. She opened her mouth to speak one of them. But none of them were believable. So she closed her mouth again. She might as well confess. She shook her head. "Locks o' hair."

"Whose hair?"

She raised her chin in challenge. "Yours and mine."

She expected him to make fun of her. He'd doubtless have a good chuckle at her expense. And just as she anticipated, he began to laugh.

But then he held aloft what he had behind his back. "Like these?"

She frowned. He was holding strands of black and auburn hair tied together with a green ribbon. Her hand went instinctively to her head as she wondered when he'd stolen a lock of her hair. "How did ye...?"

"While we were kissin'." One side of his mouth curved up in a grin. "And ye?"

She gave him a sheepish smile. "While ye were sleepin'."

He shook his head. "Come on." His eyes twinkled as he summoned her with his free hand. "We may as well get it over with."

She joined him where he stood over the well. "Do ye think 'twill work?"

"I have no idea, but 'tis worth—"

There was a sudden movement through the trees. They both froze. Someone was coming their way. Damn! The last thing Ysenda wanted was an audience for their foolishness.

But after a moment, she blinked in surprise. She recognized the lurching motion of the intruder.

Noël recognized it as well. "What the devil? Caimbeul?"

Caimbeul was struggling through the snow. His staff slipped on the slick surface. He was out of breath. But he had a wide smile on his face.

"Caimbeul!" she said, handing the locks of hair off to Noël before rushing forward to meet her brother. "Are ye all right? How did ye walk so far? And in the snow?" As far as she remembered, he'd only been to the well once before, and he'd had to ride part of the way on a vendor's cart.

He shrugged off her questions to ask his own. "What

are the two o' ye doin' here? Are ye wishin' on the well? Is that what ye're doin'?"

"Nae," she said.

"Aye," Noël said.

Ysenda frowned. She wasn't exactly proud of what they were doing.

But Caimbeul only laughed and hobbled forward, then dug something out of his satchel. For an instant, Ysenda couldn't speak.

"Is that what I think 'tis?" Noël asked.

Caimbeul grinned. "Locks o' your hair? Aye."

Ysenda blinked at the white-ribboned bundle. "I'm beginnin' to think I'm lucky I haven't been plucked bald. How did ye...?"

"Remember when I knocked ye on your arse in the courtyard?" Caimbeul asked, clearly acting the braggart. "I might have stolen a few strands while ye lay helpless."

Noël narrowed his eyes and nodded. "And ye took mine when ye had that 'accident' in the armory, didn't ye?"

"Ye said trickery was my strength." Caimbeul beamed with pride. "So what do we do now?"

It had seemed silly enough when Ysenda was thinking of making the wish by herself. Now, with three of them reciting the wish, it seemed absolutely ridiculous.

On the other hand, what did they have to lose? The fact that they all wanted the same thing touched her. And it made her more than willing to indulge the two most important men in her life.

"I suppose we weight them with rocks and drop them into the well together," she said.

Noël nodded. "That should give our wish three times the power."

Once they'd secured small rocks to each bundle, they stood together over the well.

"What are we supposed to say?" Noël asked.

"I'm not certain," Ysenda admitted. "I suppose we wish for a way to bind our two spirits together for eternity?"

"I'll do it," Caimbeul offered when they stood above the well. "I think ye should hold hands." They did. "In the name o' the unfortunate lovers who once drowned in this well, I make this Yuletide wish that the two souls to whom these locks o' hair belong to be blessed in their marriage and joined together forever and aye."

They all nodded, pleased with his choice of words. And then they dropped their tokens, one by one, into the water, where they disappeared into the inky depths.

The heavens didn't open up to let angels descend.

The air didn't stir with the breeze of faerie wings or fill with the sound of ancient pipes.

No Viking ghosts appeared.

Indeed, the moment was remarkably unremarkable.

"What do we do now?" Caimbeul asked.

Noël answered. "I suppose we wait."

As the moments crept by, Ysenda became more and more despondent. Nothing was happening. The spell wasn't working. She should have known better than to believe in magic.

After an uncomfortably long silence, she finally spoke. "Maybe we should be gettin' back."

"Do ye think it worked?" Caimbeul asked.

"Nae." The word scraped across her throat, like a sword blade on a sharpening stone.

Caimbeul's brows came together. "So what do we do now?"

Noël's chest was tight. He'd hoped he wouldn't have to answer that. He'd hoped, impossibly, that somehow the well would give him an answer. But there had been nothing.

"What we must," he decided.

Caimbeul straightened, as much as his crooked frame allowed. "Whatever happens, I'm goin' to France with ye," he blurted out. "That is," he amended, "if ye'll have me."

From the corner of his eye, Noël could see Ysenda had clenched her jaw.

He shook his head. "I can't take ye from Ysenda, Caimbeul. Ye may be her younger brother, but now that ye're grown, *she* needs *your* protection."

Caimbeul scowled, simultaneously disappointed and flattered. In the end, all he did was mutter, "I'm not her younger brother. I'm the oldest."

There was a long, melancholy silence.

Finally, Caimbeul's words sank in. Noël blinked, wondering if he'd heard wrong. "What? What did ye say?"

"I'm older than Ysenda. Three years older."

He frowned. "Ye are? And what about Cathalin?"

"I'm two years older than Cathalin."

He rattled his head. Surely that wasn't right. "Ye're the oldest?"

"Aye."

Noël closed his eyes. Was he missing something? "Ye're the *oldest?*" he repeated.

"Aye," the siblings said together.

"The oldest, as in the rightful heir to the laird?"

"Oh. Well, nae," Ysenda explained. "The laird has never...he's never claimed Caimbeul as his heir."

"Hold on." Noël's heart started to race. He didn't want to get prematurely excited. But something was awry here. "Are ye sayin' ye're the next in line?"

"In principle, aye, but—"

"Nae, nae, nae, nae," Noël interrupted. "Not in principle. In actual fact." Now his heart was pounding. This could be his answer. "Exactly why has he not claimed ye? Are ye not his son by blood?"

"I am."

"Are ye a bastard?"

"Nae."

"Why then?"

Caimbeul flushed and lowered his gaze.

Ysenda answered for him. "He's never claimed Caimbeul as his son because he's a cripple and unfit to rule."

"But he's not unfit," Noël insisted, beginning to pace eagerly now as he considered this new piece of information. "Ye saw him on the field. Not only is he bright and clever, but he can even hold his own with a sword."

Ysenda and Caimbeul stared at each other. Clearly, the thought of contesting the inheritance had never crossed their minds.

He supposed he could see why. The Highlands were so remote that a clan laird was essentially the ruler of his own domain. The Scottish king might lay down the law of the land. But the laird felt he had the power to bend that law as he saw fit.

In truth, however, laws were a matter of record. No man could alter what was written down by a king to suit his own wants or needs...not even a laird.

"It doesn't matter whether the laird wishes to claim him or not," Noël explained. "Caimbeul is his son. As long as he's fit to rule—and anyone can see he is—by law, Caimbeul is the true heir."

"So ye're sayin' the holdin' doesn't rightfully belong to Cathalin," Caimbeul mused aloud, "no matter who she weds? It belongs to me?"

"Exactly." Noël crossed his arms over his chest in satisfaction. "Which means—"

"Which means we can all have what we want," Ysenda gushed. "We can stay married and go to France. Cathalin can wed her Highlander..."

"And I can come to train with your men," Caimbeul inserted, for fear he might be excluded.

Noël gave him a slow grin. "Aye."

Caimbeul rubbed his jaw, thinking this over. Then his brow creased. "It doesn't seem possible. Do ye truly think 'twill come to pass? My father is very strong-willed. And the Highlands is a long reach for the arm o' the law."

"Which is why the king sends men like the Knights o' de Ware to enforce the law," Noël said.

"Ye'd do that?"

"Aye, o' course. Ye're one of us now."

"But what about the clan?" he asked. "I don't want war with the clan."

"They're my clan as well," Noël assured him. "When the time comes, we'll find a way to keep the peace. Ye're a clever man. Ye'll think of somethin'."

Ysenda's beautiful silver eyes shone with hope. But there was wisdom and caution in her voice. "'Twill all have to be kept a secret. If the laird suspects that Caimbeul has a claim to the holdin'..."

She didn't finish the thought. But they all knew the risk. Laird Gille wouldn't hesitate to eliminate his heir if Caimbeul proved to be...inconvenient.

"Aye," Noël said. "'Twill be a secret between the three of us."

They nodded in solemn agreement.

And then, with a soft cry of victory, Ysenda threw herself into Noël's arms.

He chuckled with pleasure and held her close.

But as their lingering embrace went on and on, Caimbeul finally rolled his eyes and turned to leave.

"Where are ye goin'?" Ysenda asked him.

"Back to the keep," he said over his shoulder. "There's somethin' I've been meanin' to do for a long while. But don't fret. By the time ye get finished...celebratin'...ye can catch up with me."

Noël bid him farewell. Then he grinned and kissed the

top of his lovely wife's head. "It looks like we'll have our whole lives to celebrate."

"Not just our lives," she murmured. "Eternity."

"It worked, didn't it?" he asked her softly. "The Viking well. It granted us our Yuletide wish."

She nodded. Then she gazed up at him. Her smile was as sweet as mulled wine. Her eyes glowed with the warmth of Christmas candles. "For ever and aye."

epilogue

Leaving her Highland home to travel south with the Knights of de Ware, Ysenda had never felt so well protected. Of course, that hadn't kept her from packing her own chain mail and weapons. Old habits were hard to break. It would be a long while before she'd grow to accept that she had an army of knights at her command and that her brother could take care of himself.

Caimbeul had certainly proved that upon their return to the castle.

Ysenda had had a lot of time to think on the way home from the well. Now that she was no longer beholden to her father, years of anger over Caimbeul's mistreatment began to fester within her. All the laird's past abuses—his mocking, violence, and cruelty—congealed into a single, hard knot of rage and injustice that stuck in her craw. With each step she took toward the castle, fury flowed hotter in her veins.

When they finally arrived at the keep to face her

father, he was alone in the great hall and deep in his cups. His drunken sneer as the three of them approached only added fuel to the almost irresistible desire Ysenda had to pay him back for all the pain he'd caused.

But she'd held her tongue as Sir Noël explained that they wished to take Caimbeul with them to France.

Her father's eyes lit up. "Ach, aye!" he crowed. "I've heard the French courts like to use dwarves and such for entertainment."

Ysenda longed to curse her father for his brutal words.

But then she heard the echo of her mother's voice. Above all, the warrior maid had taught Ysenda to maintain control of her emotions. Losing one's temper was never wise. Besides, she and Caimbeul would leave soon and likely never see the laird again. There was no point in stirring up trouble. So she tensed her jaw against the urge to fire off a biting retort.

The laird eyed Caimbeul speculatively over the top of his cup. "Or maybe ye're plannin' to sell him along the way? The lad has a decent voice. No doubt a singin' cripple could bring ye a good price."

Ysenda clenched her teeth until they hurt. But she kept mentally repeating her mother's advice. One must take a deep breath, harness all the anger, and choose one's battles wisely.

The laird took a drink and then smacked his lips. "He's probably got another five or six years o' life at most. Still, ye'll get your coin's worth."

That made Ysenda's blood boil. But no matter how

much she yearned to claw that smug smirk off of the laird's face, no matter how gratifying it would be to tear the beard from his chin, no matter how her fist ached to…

Crack!

Ysenda lifted a brow as her father's head snapped back under Caimbeul's solid punch. The laird staggered backward, dropping his cup and clutching his nose.

As Ysenda stared in wonder, Caimbeul shook his bruised knuckles. Then he grinned in satisfaction. "That's for a lifetime o' sufferin'…Da."

Those had been Caimbeul's last words to the laird, who'd shuffled off to have someone tend to his bloodied nose. Ysenda had never been prouder of her brother. And she thought their mother would agree that he'd chosen his battle wisely.

Now they were headed to France—to freedom and to family. As impossible as it seemed, Ysenda thought Caimbeul looked taller as he traveled beside his new companions-in-arms. Perhaps he no longer felt crushed by the weight of his infirmity.

As for her husband, though his men laughingly insisted Noël was the ugliest of the de Ware brothers, Ysenda could not have been happier to be wed to such a handsome, kind, noble, brilliant, and honorable man. Noël had promised that when her father died, he and his men would return with Caimbeul to help him claim the Highland holding without shedding a drop of blood.

Their path from the keep took them past the Viking well. Ysenda requested a private moment before they

continued on their journey to visit one last time. Gathering her cloak about her, she clambered across the snowdrifts until she reached the silvery stream and the crumbling stones of the ruin.

There, she ran her fingers over the ancient runes carved into the lid of the well. She whispered thanks to the lost lovers for granting her wish. Then she sent up a silent prayer of her own—that somehow, some way, no matter how long it took, the doomed couple might eventually have their own curse lifted.

By the time she returned to the company, the knights were speaking with a dozen strangers—travelers headed in the opposite direction. The band of ragged Highlanders said they were on their way to the keep of Laird Gille.

The wee lad at the fore licked his chapped lips and raised his beardless chin, boasting in his high, sweet voice that he was going to marry the bonniest lass in all of Scotland.

Ysenda's brows lifted. But she wisely held her laughter. She wished she could see her sister's face when Cathalin beheld the bridegroom she'd wanted so badly— all four feet of him.

Instead, she smiled up at Noël, whose lips were twitching with amusement. He gave her a wink, and she sighed with pleasure.

This was going to be, without a doubt, the best Yuletide ever.

The End

Thank You for Reading My Book!

Did you enjoy it? If so, I hope you'll post a review to let others know! There's no greater gift you can give an author than spreading your love of her books.

It's truly a pleasure and a privilege to be able to share my stories with you. Knowing that my words have made you laugh, sigh, or touched a secret place in your heart is what keeps the wind beneath my wings. I hope you enjoyed our brief journey together, and may ALL of your adventures have happy endings!

If you'd like to keep in touch, feel free to sign up for my monthly e-newsletter at www.glynnis.net, and you'll be the first to find out about my new releases, special discounts, prizes, promotions, and more!

If you want to keep up with my daily escapades:
Friend me at facebook.com/GlynnisCampbell
Like my Page at bit.ly/GlynnisCampbellFBPage
Follow me at twitter.com/GlynnisCampbell
And if you're a super fan, join
facebook.com/GCReadersClan

Excerpt from

my chAmpion

The Knights of de Ware Book 1

"You, Linet de Montfort," Duncan said, "are afraid of me."

Her mouth fell open, and for a moment she could think of nothing to say in her defense.

He shook his head. "You, who so boldly insulted El Gallo on the docks, who dared to confront Sombra himself, you're afraid of a lowly beggar."

"I'm not afraid," she whispered in denial. Yet deep in her heart, she knew it was true.

"You cower from me. You pretend it's disgust," he announced with self-mocking arrogance, "but I hardly think—"

"I *do* find you disgusting," she tried to convince him. But she couldn't look him in the eyes with the lie, not while that wild black curl fell across his forehead, not while his eyes shone with blue mischief.

The last thing she expected was his roar of laughter.

"Oh, aye—disgusting! And what in particular do you find disgusting?" he inquired, closing in on her again.

She eased backward. Nothing about the beggar was disgusting. Everything about him was fascinating— fascinating and dangerous.

"My nose? My eyes?" His voice softened, luring her in even as she retreated across the barn. "My mouth?"

She started to take another step away, but a spade abandoned on the stable floor tripped her up, making her stumble backward. The beggar reached out for her elbow just in time to keep her upright. But by then her back was against the planking of the stable.

"Perhaps it's my...touch that disgusts you," he said.

She was trapped now, pinned between a wall and a man whose sheer, raw masculinity rivaled the wood for strength.

"Shall I show you," he whispered, "how I kissed the crofter's wife?"

"Nay." She stiffened like a stick. Not a kiss—anything but a kiss, she thought, even as her lips tingled in anticipation. No matter what he did to her, no matter how her heart raced, she refused to bend beneath his onslaught.

"I placed my disgusting thighs here." He stepped between her legs, nudging them apart with his knee until his body was pressed intimately against hers, leaving her breathless, leaving no doubt as to his desire. "Then I placed my vulgar arms thus." With one hand, he trapped her wrists against the solid wall of his chest, slipping the other gently around her throat. His fingers were like Lucca silk against her skin as they slid up the side of her neck and tangled in the curls at the back of her head.

Her breath grew shallow. She dared not look at him.

"Then," he breathed against the corner of her mouth, "I pressed my crude...lips...so."

His mouth closed over hers as if she were a chalice of sweet wine, his tongue flicking lightly along the rim of her lips, tasting her, tempting her. She closed her eyes tightly, fighting her own desires, willing the embers glowing inside her to subside. But it was useless. His kiss stole the very thoughts from her brain.

For one brief moment, he withdrew, granting her respite from the chaotic emotions clouding her mind. For an instant, she could almost think.

Then he kissed her again. This time he embraced her completely, plundering her senses, devouring her with all the ardor of a starving man. Her blood rushed through her ears, as if he'd summoned it all the way from her toes. Every inch of her skin responded to his touch like iron filings awakening to a lodestone.

Even when he pulled away at last, when his thumb brushed her bottom lip, she felt the lingering molten heat of his kiss. She could no more silence the ragged sigh that slipped out between her teeth, the sigh that pleaded for more, than she could stop the tides.

She never meant to surrender. But once she felt the demand of his searching mouth, once the muscles of his body contoured themselves to her, all care ceased. She knew only that she wanted...something more.

Duncan knew what she wanted. And he fully intended to appease her. He released her hands—hands grown limp in his—to wrap one possessive arm around her back. Then, to his amazement, before he could muster his forces for another onslaught, the hungry little vixen threw herself with abandon against him, into a kiss of her own making. She crushed her breasts against his ribs and opened her mouth to him, exploring his shoulders, his face, his hair with frenzied hands.

And he lost control.

Never, *never* had it happened before. He'd made love to dozens of women, kissed scores more. God's bones, the de Ware brothers were the envy of the barony when it came to seduction. But always he was in control. It was he who set the pace, planned each move, each word, and knew the moment of surrender. He always knew how far he could go and how to gracefully back away. Now, for the first time, he was utterly and completely powerless to stop himself.

About the Author

I'm a *USA Today* bestselling author of swashbuckling action-adventure historical romances, mostly set in Scotland, with over a dozen award-winning books published in six languages.

But before my role as a medieval matchmaker, I sang in *The Pinups,* an all-girl band on CBS Records, and provided voices for the MTV animated series *The Maxx,* Blizzard's *Diablo* and *Starcraft* video games, and *Star Wars* audiobooks.

I'm the wife of a rock star (if you want to know which one, contact me) and the mother of two young adults. I do my best writing on cruise ships, in Scottish castles, on my husband's tour bus, and at home in my sunny southern California garden.

I love transporting readers to a place where the bold heroes have endearing flaws, the women are stronger than they look, the land is lush and untamed, and chivalry is alive and well!

I'm always delighted to hear from my readers, so please feel free to email me at glynnis@glynnis.net. And if you're a super-fan who would like to join my inner circle, sign up at http://www.facebook.com/GCReadersClan, where you'll get glimpses behind the scenes, sneak peeks of works-in-progress, and extra special surprises!

CPSIA information can be obtained at www.ICGtesting.com
Printed in the USA
BVOW05s1540171215

430523BV00051B/95/P